being human
Chasers

being human
CHASERS

Mark Michalowski

BOOKS

Being Human is a Touchpaper TV production for BBC Three
Executive Producers: Toby Whithouse and Rob Pursey

Original series created by Toby Whithouse and broadcast on BBC Television.
'Being Human' and the Being Human logo are trademarks of the
British Broadcasting Corporation and are used under licence

10 9 8 7 6 5 4 3 2 1

Published in 2010 by BBC Books, an imprint of Ebury Publishing.
A Random House Group Company.

The Random House Group Ltd Reg. No. 954009.
Addresses for companies within the Random House Group can be found at
www.randomhouse.co.uk.

A CIP catalogue record for this book is available from the British Library.

ISBN 978 1 846 07899 6

The Random House Group Limited supports the Forest Stewardship Council
(FSC), the leading international forest certification organisation. All our titles
that are printed on Greenpeace approved FSC certified paper carry the FSC
logo. Our paper procurement policy can be found at www.rbooks.co.uk/
environment

Series Editor: Steve Tribe
Cover design by Lee Binding © Woodlands Books, 2010

Printed and bound in Great Britain by CPI Cox and Wyman, Reading, RG1 8EX

To buy books by your favourite authors and register for offers,
visit www.rbooks.co.uk

For Steve Tribe,
the unsung hero

Paris, New Year's Eve, 1951
Crowds.

Don't you just love 'em.

All that warmth and noise and flesh and blood.

And where better to see the New Year in than on the Champs Elysées, swimming in a sea of humanity, a shark cruising for a meal. Or maybe just a light snack. Snaking my way through them all, flashing a smile, 'Bonjour!', 'Bonne année!', a wink – and a deep breath in, tasting the air like a snake with its tongue.

And then moving on.

It's too soon to bring this night to an end. I'm here for a buffet, not a sit-down meal. But first I want to smell the dishes, get my juices flowing. Check out what's on the menu.

OK, enough culinary metaphors. I liked the one with the

shark better. But then I would, wouldn't I? I'm not a chef in some poncey restaurant, sampling the ingredients just enough to know what they'll bring to the final dish. I'm here to eat. And I'm looking for good old-fashioned meat-and-two-veg, not some miniature concoction served on an oversized plate. Food I can get my teeth into.

Ha – I'm back to the culinary thing again, aren't I? Maybe that's my subconscious telling me I should have been a chef and not… what I am. Not that it's exactly a career choice. Not that the two are mutually exclusive. I heard about one vampire – there, I've said it! The V-word that so many of us seem to avoid at every opportunity. Vampire! Vampire vampire vampire! Ha! – who approached his kills like a chef. Italian, as it turned out (better not tell the Frenchies that – they'd hate that, wouldn't they?). He always organised multiple kills, picking the victims for their 'unique qualities', blending them in his head – and, no doubt, in his mouth – to create something special, something marvellous.

Nah, that's not me. Don't get me wrong – I can be fussy about who I kill. Well, I'm attractive enough to be able to pick and choose. Sometimes I pity the ones who achieved Nirvana when they were old: stuck like that, never changing, always being old. Wonder if it rankles with them? I like to think – on the few occasions that I 'do my duty' and bring another one into the fold – that I'm doing it humanely: the younger, prettier ones. The ones that have so much more to gain from immortality. It was lucky it happened to me when it did, isn't it? Imagine all the skulking around and seediness it must take to drink vibrant young blood when you have the face of a 70-year-old. But there are fewer and fewer of them about, strange as that might seem. Although

I think the war's balanced that one up a bit, hasn't it? You don't see so many young men on the streets, more single young women. I think the old ones are just that bit easier to kill – to stake, behead, whatever – than us youngsters. Physically younger, obviously: you never can tell the age of the mind behind a vampire's eyes, trust me. And as more of us convert younger, sexy, attractive ones and the oldies are slowly dying off, we truly are becoming the Beautiful People.

And talking of beautiful people…

Now she's nice. Her there, looking around, checking her watch. 11.30. Still half an hour to go until midnight, but the Champs Elysées is absolutely packed. From side to side, and as far down as I can see without standing on something. There's a slight natural dip to it that means, if you stand on your toes, you get a great view – a thick, thick carpet of humanity, all the way from the Eiffel Tower down to the Arc de Triomphe.

Oh boy, a deep breath in – and it's like the best smell ever. I don't know if it's pheromones or sweat or breath or just carbon dioxide. Or if it's something weird and supernatural. I can't even describe it – it's like a whole new scent, like a new colour in the rainbow. How d'you describe that to someone?

But yes, she's nice. Waiting for friends, wrapped up in a big, rough-looking coat. Maybe a soldier's coat – probably a genuine one, thinking about it. Maybe she's waiting for her man. Maybe just friends. I like the beret – that is so French. Blonde curls, cute little nose. Now she's cupping her hands together and blowing into them.

She sees me looking and I smile and shrug myself into a

'Isn't it cold?' posture and she smiles back. And then she looks away sharply, like she thinks she's doing something wrong. But I keep my eyes on her, and after she's made a very deliberate effort to scan the crowd, she glances back at me.

I hold up the gloves that I've just taken from my pocket and grin.

And then, hoping my smile doesn't look too shark-like, I launch myself through the river of humanity that surrounds me, on course for my supper.

Predator and prey.

Chapter
ONE

'Kaz!' said Mitchell.

Standing in the street, under a rainbow umbrella – despite the complete and total absence of rain – was Kaz. Her face was flushed, and she looked as if she'd been running.

Kaz did a funny little dance as she struggled to catch her breath and said something that sounded like 'Jaw'.

'Jaw?' echoed Mitchell.

'George,' said Kaz, more clearly this time.

'Mitchell,' beamed Mitchell.

'No. George. Where is he?' said Kaz. 'Need to see George. He's…'

Mitchell watched her take another big, gulping breath.

'George is going to be a daddy!' she told him.

11

Mitchell boggled. He took a step back and waved her in. She struggled with the umbrella.

Annie rolled her eyes as the new arrival entered the house. Kaz. One of George's lesbian friends. The lesbian friend who apparently thought that George and Mitchell were a couple. The lesbian friend whose girlfriend, Gail, had got on *surprisingly* well with George on the road protest the other day. The lesbian friend to whom Annie was totally invisible. Literally.

'Don't tell him, yeah?,' Kaz said to Mitchell. 'This is, like, personal – OK?' Without waiting for an answer, she pushed past the still-boggling Mitchell and made a beeline for the kitchen doorway and George, who was walking into the living room. He stopped and let her hug him.

There was an awkwardness to George in situations like this: big, chunky and just a little uncoordinated (never mind the glasses and the sticky-out ears), George was like a kid who had been brought up to require permission for everything. There was something simultaneously endearing and sad about it, Annie thought.

George pulled back, looked down at the umbrella and then out of the door.

'It's not raining,' he said.

'I know,' Kaz rolled her eyes, as George took the brolly from her and stood it in the corner. 'Only I've just had my hair braided, see, and it's like, you know, when you have a perm and you mustn't get it wet or it'll go all…' She mimed a sudden, explosive Afro.

'Right,' said George.

12

Annie pulled a face, almost pleased that Kaz couldn't see her. She looked over at Mitchell. He was making frantic gestures at her and seemed to be mouthing *What the hell's going on?!* Annie shrugged and turned back to watch the show.

'I'd kill for a cuppa,' Kaz said, shucking off her coat. It smelled of wet dog, despite being totally dry. Like the rest of Kaz's outfit, it was what she'd have called 'charity shop chic'. Annie would have said 'tramp'. George handed it to Mitchell who, holding it at arm's length, draped it over the back of a chair whilst George led Kaz across the lounge.

'I only drink herbal and fruit teas,' Kaz called over her shoulder.

'Earl Grey with a splash of Ribena,' whispered Annie to Mitchell. She followed the other two, leaving Mitchell to do the honours.

With an unnecessarily loud 'Oof!', Kaz fell back onto the sofa and began unbuttoning her cardigan. Annie spotted at least two more under there.

'You wouldn't believe what a day I've been having,' said Kaz. She paused in her undressing and looked round the room. 'You should decorate in here.'

'We should?' Mitchell asked. 'And that's what you've come all this way to tell George, is it, Kaz?'

George frowned. 'Mitchell, Kaz is our *guest*…'

'You need my friend Esme,' Kaz barrelled on, returning to the task of de-layering herself. 'Like, she's only the best feng shui person in Bristol.'

'And that's what we need, is it?' asked Mitchell. 'Not, say, you telling George what's brought you here?'

'Totally.' Kaz shuddered exaggeratedly. 'This place is like… Brrrrrrr!'

'That'll be me, I expect,' Annie said, knowing full well that Kaz couldn't hear her. 'The resident undead.' She pulled a face. 'Maybe *that*'s what's been keeping me here – the sofa's in the wrong place and we need a fish tank. Problem solved.'

'There's a bad vibe here,' Kaz continued. 'Not you two, obviously.' She looked around, eyes narrowed, as if searching for something. She hunched her shoulders. 'Unsettled. Yeah, definitely unsettled. D'you want Esme's number?'

'We'll have a think,' George said. 'Anyway, to what do we owe the pleasure?'

'Finally,' breathed Mitchell.

'Just thought I'd come and say hello to my favourite couple…' wheedled Kaz.

George rolled his eyes. 'Kaz…'

Suddenly Mitchell was there next to him, his arm draped across his shoulder.

'Mitchell!' George shrugged him off.

'Intimacy issues, yeah?' said Kaz with a wink.

'No,' replied George, scowling at Mitchell. 'Not-being-gay issues.'

Kaz just raised an eyebrow.

'She's right though,' Annie said from the kitchen. 'You do make a lovely couple. Tea's up – you might want to bring her ladyship's – unless we think it would be fun to freak her out with floating cups…'

Kaz began tugging off her purple pixie boots as Mitchell fetched the tea. Annie followed him in to see

Kaz rooting around in her bag and pulling out a little tin with a rainbow on it.

'Oh, not those herbal things,' moaned Annie. 'They smell like burning incontinence pants. George – tell her she can't smoke in here. It's bad for...' She tailed off, realising that any appeal on the grounds of her health was likely to be completely ignored.

'So, Kaz...' Mitchell gave a forced smile. 'You have something to tell us? Something to say to George?'

George opened his mouth to say something, but Kaz didn't give him the chance.

'Well,' she said, tucking her feet under her bum and leaning forward. 'You'll never guess...'

There was a pause. George shrugged.

'Go on,' urged Kaz, starting to roll one of her vile little cigarettes – hedge clippings and dung, Annie suspected. 'Guess!'

'Gail's realised what a shallow, self-centred, pseudo-hippy you are?' suggested Annie, perching herself on the arm of a chair.

'Erm... you've been promoted?' ventured George. Kaz worked on reception in Intensive Care, although from what Annie had heard, 'worked' was something of an exaggeration.

'Yeah,' said Kaz scornfully. 'Right. Like those fascists would recognise true talent when they saw it. What's that new administrator's name?'

'Guffy?' said Mitchell. 'Dr McGough.'

Kaz nodded, her lip curling into a sneer. 'I think he's got a thing for me, yeah?'

Annie laughed out loud, and both Mitchell and

George turned to look at her before they could stop themselves.

'Really?' asked George, trying to sound like he took the suggestion sensibly.

'Too right – I keep catching him looking at me. And I was in the lift with him yesterday, right, and he started talking to me – asking me how I was getting on and all that stuff.' She gave another shudder, took a sip of her 'fruit tea' and finished rolling her ciggie.

As she lit up, George began to cough profusely. Annie just felt sick.

'Should get that cough looked at,' said Kaz, flapping the smoke away from herself. 'Probably picked up that MENSA thing from work.'

'MRSA,' Mitchell corrected her. She glared at him.

'I give up,' George said.

'Give up what?'

'I give up – what's happened?'

Kaz stared at him blankly for a moment – before realising what he was on about. 'Oh!'

'Yeah, Kaz,' said Mitchell. 'I think we'd *all* like to hear what's brought you here.'

She looked across at him.

'What?' said Mitchell.

'It's, like, private, yeah?'

'Oh, right.' Mitchell stood up. 'I'll be… erm.' He looked at his watch. 'Oh, is that the time? Better get into work, then.'

'You're not on till later,' Annie said, annoyed that Kaz was driving Mitchell out of his own home.

An awkward silence descended on the room as

Mitchell faffed around looking for his keys and mobile and ID badge. Kaz puffed away on her cigarette, filling the air with disgusting, yellowy smoke, before stubbing it out in an empty mug.

'Keep an eye on her,' Mitchell whispered to Annie as he left, giving Kaz a cheery goodbye wave. 'You know what a sucker George is. Don't let her drag him into anything stupid.'

'Right,' Kaz said as the door closed and Annie came back. She took a swig of tea. 'You,' she said to George with a mischievous twinkle in her eye, 'are gonna be, like, *soooo* pleased, yeah?'

'I am?'

'Too right!' She leaned forward. 'You, Georgie-boy, are gonna be a *daddy*!'

The morning was crisp and bright and, despite the draining presence of Kaz, Mitchell felt a definite spring in his step. Maybe it was the fact that Gemma had finally gone; maybe it was the fact that Herrick had finally *finally* gone; or maybe it was, simply, that it was a beautiful morning.

Mitchell paused and looked back at the house. It looked so... *innocent*. Just an odd-shaped terrace on the corner of a mundane street. Innocent. An odd word to use for a house – especially considering the things that it had seen. But, right now, that's just how it felt. Mitchell had a feeling that it was going to be a good day. Taking a deep lungful of autumn air, he set off in the direction of Victoria Park.

*

'You're sacked!'

'What?' Mitchell gawped and spun round, catching his elbow painfully on the locker door.

It was Mossy – Trevor Moss, another orderly, rooting around in his own locker. He pocketed his ciggies and lighter.

'The bowling team,' Mossy said in answer to Mitchell's expression. He paused, waiting for a response. 'Last night? Bowling? You signed up three weeks ago, remember. And how many times have you actually bothered to turn up?'

Mitchell's shoulders sagged.

'Sorry about that,' he said, trying to pour oil on waters that he could already see boiling. 'Been a bit of a busy time.'

'Sfine,' said Mossy, shutting his locker. 'Just that Kate wanted to join and I had to say no.'

'Sorry,' Mitchell said again.

'Not me you should apologise to,' Mossy sniffed.

'I'll have a word with her.'

'You do that,' said Mossy over his shoulder. And he was gone.

Good start, thought Mitchell, changing into his work gear and clipping his badge on. He glanced at the photo, as he did every time he wore it: a remarkable likeness. Quite how Herrick had managed to find such a good doppelgänger he didn't know. *Herrick.* Mitchell sighed. He didn't doubt that George's seeing-off of Herrick had been a good thing but, now that the dust had settled, he had a growing sense of unease about it all. Like when you first spot a dangling thread on

a favourite jumper, and have a little tug at it. Maybe
you get the nail scissors out and clip it off. But then,
a few weeks later, it's back, so you give it another
pull. And before you know it, the whole thing starts
unravelling.

Mitchell wondered how long it'd be before the local
vampire community ('vampire community'? Was there
really such a thing?) started falling apart with only the
local small fry like Albert to hold it all together. Little
things like ID photos: back when it had all started, all
those years ago, Mitchell hadn't had to worry about
technology tripping him up. But now – with cameras,
mobile phones, CCTV, webcams everywhere, every
journey outside the four walls of the house was asking
for trouble. He rarely went to parties – there was
always someone guaranteed to pull out a camera and
demand a group shot; or, worse, someone popping up
out of nowhere and snapping him without any notice.
Sooner or later, people were going to catch on: there
were only so many times he could grab the camera
under the pretext of wanting to see the pic first, and
then 'accidentally' deleting it. The road protest had
been a case in point – all that fuss getting hold of Gavin
Foot's camera. The journalist had probably been a little
bit surprised to find a great big wodge of nothing in his
photos. And it was one of the reasons Mitchell hadn't
made any effort to keep his promise to Mossy and turn
up for bowling: after he'd agreed, Mossy had pointed
out last year's team photo in the staff rec room. How
would he ever get out of that?

He'd never given it much thought before, but it

was just one more small way in which vampires went unnoticed. Literally *unseen*.

He looked down at his ID card again – if he lost it, what would he do? Where would he find someone that looked enough like him and who'd stand in for him? At least, he thought, the photo was never going to date – one reason he did his best, with Annie's help, to keep his hair and stubble the same. Continuity.

As he slammed the locker door shut, he realised that without Herrick, in many ways the world was a more dangerous place for him.

Damn.

And it had started out such a lovely day.

'Morning handsome!' called Sarah from behind her desk as Mitchell slouched through. He managed a half-arsed smile.

'Mossy caught up with you, then?'

Mitchell's shoulders drooped as he perched his bum on the reception desk. Sarah was one of the bowling team, and it had been partly down to her that he'd eventually relented and said yes. She was bright and cheery and just the teensiest bit sexy.

'I'm sacked, apparently,' he said.

Sarah raised an eyebrow.

'Well, he likes his little fix of power. Reckon it'll be Meera next. She's rubbish, and Mossy has his eye on the trophy – and Haematology have got Ollie Clarke and he's *good*.' Sarah paused. 'Hey – maybe George'd like to come along.'

Yeah, thought Mitchell. George. Bowling. Actually,

maybe it wasn't such a bad idea. He needed more fun, more friends.

'I'll ask him – don't count on it, though – a bit too much like fun for George.'

'Well, ask him anyway. He should get out more – you both should…' She tailed off as the new hospital administrator, Dr McGough, swooshed in through the main doors, nodded at the two of them, and headed on into the hospital.

'I keep telling him,' Mitchell said, 'but you know George. Always has to be fretting about something or other. Wouldn't be George otherwise. Anyway,' he stood up. 'Better do some work – old Guffy there just gave me the evil eye.' He leaned in close to Sarah and glared at her as sinisterly as he could.

Sarah snorted. 'You're rubbish at that – my nan looks more evil than you, and she doesn't even have her own teeth.'

Mitchell winked. 'Maybe that's where I'm going wrong.' He ostentatiously licked his right canine.

You're going to have to stop doing that, Mitchell told himself sternly as soon as he was round the corner. One day it was going to go too far. As any alcoholic knows, you don't go down the booze aisle in Tesco sniffing the labels on the bottles. If he really was going to find a way to kick his own addiction, he had to stop flirting. But it was hard. *Very* hard. He suddenly craved a cigarette – something tangible and physical, something to take his mind off his other craving.

'Sorry, mate!'

A voice suddenly brought him out of his reverie as a swinging door nearly smacked him in the face. It was only the quick action of the voice's owner that stopped Mitchell from rediscovering the taste of his own blood. The man held the door open and Mitchell nodded his thanks.

'Looking for, um, Oncology,' said the man. He gestured down the corridor. 'This way, is it?'

He was a bit paunchy, dressed head-to-toe in black (which exacerbated his pallor) with a bootlace tie and silver wing-tips on his collar. On anyone younger, it might have looked stylish. On this guy – mid 40s, Mitchell guessed – it just looked a bit sad. His hair was thinning – not quite McGough-thin, but getting there – and greased straight back over his head. Mitchell wasn't the least bit surprised to catch sight of a tiny, stubby ponytail, tied with a black rubber band.

'Yeah, straight on, then first left and follow the signs. And cheers,' he added, remembering how the man had stopped the door from hitting him in the face.

'No worries, mate,' the man said. 'Your lady friend back there might not be so keen on you with a broken nose and a black eye.'

'Lady friend?' *Sarah*. 'Oh,' said Mitchell. 'We just work together.'

The man laughed as the two of them headed off down the corridor. 'Reckon she thinks it's a bit more than that. Trust me – I know the signs.'

Mitchell just smiled awkwardly. He wasn't sure he wanted to be discussing his love life – or lack of – with a complete stranger. Particularly a complete stranger with silver wing-tips. At the first intersection, Mitchell thanked the man again and turned left.

'See ya later,' the man called to Mitchell.

Yeah, thought Mitchell. *Later.*

'Got any more of that tea?' asked Kaz, reaching across for her tobacco tin. She caught sight of George's expression. 'What? It's safe – I've looked on the internet and everything.'

'Not the tobacco,' said George patiently, his mind still whirring, catching up on what Kaz had just said. 'The daddy thing.'

'Yeah,' Kaz said, all fired up again. 'Cool, eh?'

George shook his head. 'What are you talking about?'

'Me and Gail – remember? You said you'd do anything you could to help.' She stared at him. 'With *the baby*.'

'Just saying "the baby" isn't helping,' snapped George. He glanced over at Annie who was perched on the arm of the sofa, gawping at him, clearly enjoying his discomfort.

'Have you two…?' Annie pointed at him, and then at Kaz, and then wiggled her finger between the two of them.

'No!'

'What?' said Kaz. 'But you said—'

'No, no, I didn't mean "no",' waffled George. Even after all this time, he still hadn't got the hang of having three-way conversations with normal people and a ghost.

23

'But you just said "no".'

'I wasn't…' George sighed and pushed his glasses back up his nose. 'I meant… I meant I didn't know you were…' He stopped. *Start again*. 'What d'you mean, *I'm* going to be a daddy?'

'Me and Gail, yeah – we've decided.'

'Decided to have a baby,' ventured George.

'Yeah. I told you we were going to go for IVF and all that, remember. And you said if there was, like, anything you could do to help…'

Kaz raised her eyebrows, prompting him.

'So…' ventured George tentatively. 'You're, what… pregnant?'

Kaz pulled a horrified face. 'No thank you! I did a test in *Cosmo* – I'm not a natural mother.'

'Not a natural anything,' muttered Annie.

'So *Gail's* pregnant.'

Kaz rolled her eyes as if dealing with a particularly slow child. 'Not yet she's not.'

The penny dropped.

'Oh,' said George.

'Oh,' echoed Annie.

'Yeah!' Kaz grinned. 'Cool, yeah?'

'I,' said George slowly, wanting to make sure he wasn't still misunderstanding, 'am going to be the father of Gail's baby.'

'Of *our* baby,' Kaz corrected him, rolling another ciggie. 'No offence, yeah, but it's like me and Gail's. You're…' Kaz ran out of words. 'You're gonna be her uncle.'

'Her uncle,' George said slowly.

'But really,' Kaz leaned closer and winked, 'you'll be her dad, obviously.'

'Obviously,' Annie said, as a look of something halfway between disbelief and horror spread across his face. 'George... Kitchen. Now.'

'What?'

'Her dad,' repeated Kaz.

'Yes, yes...' George suddenly felt very hot and slightly sick.

'Kitchen,' Annie said again, standing up.

'I'll, erm, get you another tea,' George said as Kaz started fiddling with the roach for her roll-up.

'Got any organic sugar?'

'Um, I'll have a look.'

George took Kaz's mug and followed Annie into the kitchen.

'What the hell was that all about?' demanded Annie once they were out of earshot.

'Ssssh!' said George.

'She can't hear me, George. I'm dead, remember. Like you seem to be – from the neck up at any rate. *Daddy*?'

George filled the kettle. 'She's just got hold of the wrong end of the stick.'

'You mean turkey baster.'

'What?'

Annie arched an eyebrow.

George thought for a second. 'Oh...'

'When did you tell the Stupidest Hobo in there that you'd be the father to her devil child?'

'I didn't,' hissed George, trying to keep his voice

down. He reached out and put the radio on, hoping it'd cover the sound of his conversation. 'Baby Love' blared out.

'Well maybe I'm not following the conversation very well, but that's certainly the idea that *she's* got.'

'She must have, um, misunderstood.'

'Misunderstood what? *Yes, I'd be happy to supply some of my…*' Annie flapped her hands '*… stuff so that you and your girlfriend can get yourselves a new little plaything*? That kind of misunderstanding?'

'It's OK,' said George. 'I'll sort it out. They obviously just want me to be a godfather or something.'

'Yeah,' agreed Annie, pulling a serious face. 'That's obviously what they're thinking. George! You've got to get back in there and put her straight.'

George pulled a *ha-ha* face.

'And not like that,' Annie added. 'Not unless you're planning on actually "doing the job" yourself.'

George just boggled at her.

'Who you talking to?' came Kaz's voice.

'The radio,' said George without thinking.

'You're talking to the radio?'

'It's a… phone-in,' George finished lamely, wishing he hadn't even started the sentence.

'Oh, right,' said Kaz, clearly mollified.

'Thank God it's Gail who's having the baby,' said Annie. 'There's one set of genes you don't want polluting the pool.'

'There's nothing wrong with her,' George said, trying to remember how to make Kaz's fruit tea.

Annie snorted and elbowed him out of the way,

reaching for the Earl Grey. 'She's a halfwit!'

'She's lovely.'

'Who's lovely?'

George and Annie turned to see Kaz, standing in the opening to the lounge and struggling with her cigarette lighter.

'What?'

'Who's lovely?' Kaz looked puzzled. 'I thought you were, like, on the phone.' She stared at George. 'On the radio, yeah? The phone-in.'

'Oh, right, yes. Gloria Hunniford.'

It was Annie's turn to boggle.

'You know,' she said, heading off into the lounge. 'I'm not sure whose genes are the most dodgy – hers or yours.'

'She's a fascist,' said Kaz, and without further comment, went back to the sofa to continue her struggle with her cigarette lighter.

Realising that Kaz meant Gloria Hunniford and not Annie, George followed her in with the tea – only to discover Annie, leaning over her: every time Kaz managed to get a flame out of the lighter, Annie blew it out. Over and over.

'It's like watching a cat with a ball of wool,' Annie grinned as Kaz took a moment to shake the lighter and peer into it.

'You got a lighter, George? This one's acting up.'

'You should be giving up, you know,' George said. 'Those things. When Gail's pregnant…'

Kaz waved vaguely. 'She's cool. Did you know that smokers are less likely to get Alzheimer's?'

'That,' said George, putting Kaz's tea down, 'is because they die of lung cancer before they're old enough to get Alzheimer's.'

Kaz threw him a disdainful look. 'You're just a slave to conventional medical thinking, you are.'

'I work in a hospital,' George pointed out. '*You* work in a hospital. I'd have thought that Intensive Care would put you off smoking for life.'

'Yeah,' said Kaz, finally – despite Annie's best efforts – getting her foul cigarette lit. 'Whatever.' She settled back on the sofa and patted the seat beside her. George cautiously sat down.

'We've got plans to make,' Kaz said.

'Have we?'

'Too right we have, yeah! Now… you know me and Gail were looking into IVF?'

George nodded cautiously.

'Bollocks,' Kaz said with a dismissive wave. 'Have you any idea how many hoops you have to jump through?'

George shook his head.

'Too many.' She coughed on a lungful of smoke. 'And I told her: "Gail, your chakras are all over the place as it is. All that poking about and tests and stuff will just make you worse."'

'So…'

'So why be a dog and…' Kaz paused. 'Bark at yourself.'

'You're getting a dog? Is that sensible if you're thinking of—'

'No no! I mean why go through all of that when we

have our own dog – sorry. Not that, like, you're a dog or anything.'

George felt himself begin to flush.

'What I mean is… You offered to help, right?'

George opened his mouth to explain that actually *being* the father wasn't quite what he had in mind; that he was thinking more along the lines of helping to bring the child up, take it to the zoo, be a godfather. That sort of thing.

But all that came out was: 'Yes.'

He caught sight of Annie's frustrated face and deliberately didn't make eye contact.

'So,' Kaz said, suddenly bright. 'There you are! Gail's got a thing off the internet, yeah? For her timings.'

'Timings?'

'Her temperature and mucous and all that.' She pulled a pukey face. 'A calendar thing that'll work out when she's most fertile. Then all you have to do is…' Kaz raised her eyebrows and glanced down at George's crotch. 'You know, *the thing*, and Bob's your uncle. Well,' she grinned. 'George is your daddy! How easy could it be, right?'

'Yeah,' said George, feeling like he'd been hit in the face with a small table. 'Easy. Right.'

Chapter
Two

Mitchell's morning plodded on.

What had started out as a bright, breezy day had turned into just another day of drudgery. It had gone downhill with Mossy and the bowling, and had got marginally worse with the all-in-black bloke's comments about Sarah. Did she really have a thing for him? He'd always assumed, he pondered, as he headed off to collect someone for their chemotherapy, that she was just flirting. Maybe he'd been so long without a girlfriend that he'd started to forget what the signs were.

The problem was that he could never disentangle 'normal' feelings for someone from... from *the hunger*. No matter how much he forced it to the back of his head, tied it up and slammed the door on it, *the hunger* was always there, waiting, biding its time. Sometimes it'd be quiet for days and he'd forget all about it. And then, out of nowhere, he'd hear it scratching at the door. *Skrikk skrikk skrikk*. Like nails on a blackboard. *I'm here, Mitchell*, it'd whisper. *Don't forget me, cos I won't forget you*.

And just when he thought he might be getting to know someone properly, normally, he'd hear it whispering again, reminding him of Lauren and all the others, how he could never really let himself go. Played havoc with his social life – or lack of. There were too many pitfalls, too many traps. He couldn't afford to lose control, to let his guard slip.

'This is Mr Edwards,' said the ward sister as Mitchell arrived with the wheelchair. 'Off for a spot of chemo, aren't you, Mr Edwards?'

She smiled brightly at the pale bag of sticks perched on the bed. Mitchell reckoned he was in his late fifties, but it was hard to tell: the man's pallid face hung in unhealthy folds, despite his skinniness. He smiled weakly at Mitchell. The nurse handed over the man's records.

'Just Charlie'll be fine,' he said.

'I'll see what I can do,' Mitchell winked. 'But I think you'll have to stick with the chemo.'

Charlie began to laugh and doubled up as a thin, rattly cough took over his body.

The nurse threw Mitchell a disapproving look.

'Well that's not going to help, is it?' she said through pursed lips.

'She could do with something to loosen her up,' Charlie said as Mitchell helped the old man into the

32

wheelchair and checked his dressing gown wasn't tangled up in the wheels.

'Not an easy job,' Mitchell defended her. 'She's probably been on all night.'

'She bloody hasn't – she only came on half an hour ago. She's always like that.'

They trundled along in silence for a few minutes, Charlie clearly struggling not to cough.

'What is it, then?' Mitchell asked.

'Me? Guess!'

'Lungs?'

'And the rest – started out in me lungs, now I've got the buggers everywhere.'

Mitchell slipped into autopilot – dealing with terminally ill patients was an everyday occurrence for him, and he'd learned the patter.

'They're doing their best for you.'

'Happen,' agreed Charlie, unconvincingly. 'Not me I'm bothered about.' He stopped. 'No, it *is* me. My daughter's just got pregnant with her first 'un.'

'Congratulations! You're going to be a granddad, then.'

'If I live to see it.' There was a very bitter edge to Charlie's voice. An edge that Mitchell had heard a hundred times before. 'That's what I mean – I could say I want to hang around for the sake of Julie and the little 'un. But if I'm being honest, it's for me.' He tipped his head back to look up at Mitchell. 'I'd just like to see him – or her – y'know, before I go.'

'Only nine months,' Mitchell said. 'Bet you can hang on that long, can't you?'

'The way my consultant's talking, I'm gonna be lucky to see Christmas.'

With practised ease, Mitchell said nothing.

'You got kids, then?' Charlie asked as they entered the lift.

'Me?' Mitchell laughed. 'Nah.'

'Not one of them queers, are you? No offence or nothing. Just, like, with the hair and everything.'

'No,' Mitchell had to laugh. 'I'm not. And I don't think you should let anyone hear you saying that, Charlie. The word is "gay".'

'What's so gay about 'em? Don't get me wrong – nothing against 'em. But nowt wrong with the word queer, is there? They even call 'emselves it. Seen it on the telly.'

Mitchell held back from a discussion about political correctness. *Life's too short.*

'So how come you don't have kids, then?' Charlie didn't seem to want to let it go. Maybe that's what happened when you were staring death in the face – you started to make an effort.

Mitchell wheeled out his pat response: 'Not met a woman who'd put up with me. I'm an acquired taste.'

The lift doors slid open.

'Don't want to leave it too long,' Charlie said. 'If I'd had Julie a couple of years earlier…' He stopped and looked up again. 'You don't know what might happen to you.'

Oh, thought Mitchell. *I think I do. Nothing. Nothing's going to happen to me. No cancer. No heart attack. No stroke. Nothing.*

Annie had decided that Kaz had been there quite long enough and that she really needed to speak to George about all this baby business before the dopey woman pulled out some sort of contract and got him to sign on the dotted line. It felt a bit like those *Watchdog* programmes where a concealed camera showed a greasy salesman selling some old dear a £5,000 bed that she neither needed nor could afford. Even standing right behind Kaz and pulling faces when George looked at her wasn't getting the message across.

'George,' she said firmly as Kaz started to talk about names for 'her daughter' (the idea that it might, just possibly, be a boy, didn't seem to have occurred to her. Annie wouldn't have put it past Kaz to be there at the birth with a pair of nail scissors up her sleeves, just to make sure...)

George glared at her.

'We need to talk about this.'

He ignored her.

'I could start moving things around, you know,' Annie warned, stretching out her hands and giving her fingers a wiggly warm-up. 'Put the willies up her – oh, bad choice of words. Look, you can't just say yes to this without talking it through with me and Mitchell.'

But of course he could, she told herself. This was George's life, George's... sperm. He could do what he wanted with it.

Suddenly there was a muffled tune playing.

'What's that?' asked Annie.

Kaz dived for her bag and pulled out her mobile – it was playing a dreadfully tinny rendition of 'Sisters Are Doin' It For Themselves'. Annie rolled her eyes and George scowled at her.

'Hiya babes,' said Kaz in a baby voice. Annie stuck her fingers in her mouth. George scowled again. 'Yeah, I'm here already. Yeah…' She looked up at George and winked. 'Sorry – I couldn't wait… Yeah. Yeah. I know, babes. I know. But it's all good, yeah?'

George gestured towards the kitchen and left Kaz to chat. Annie followed at speed.

'Look,' she said, ultra-reasonable. 'I know this is your… your stuff.'

'Sperm, Annie. It's called sperm. Not a difficult word to say – look: suh-puh-er-mm.'

'I meant,' said Annie, folding her arms, 'it's your *business*.'

'Oh,' said George. 'Right.'

'But don't you think you should talk to me and Mitchell about it?'

'Why? It's not your baby.'

'It's not just about you – and even if it were, we're your friends, George. For God's sake, don't commit yourself to something like this before you've thought it through.'

'You need to stop this, yeah,' said Kaz suddenly. She was standing there, putting her mobile back in her bag.

'This what?' said George.

'This talking to yourself. It's not normal.' She stopped and her eyes widened. 'You're not, like, mental or anything are you? Only you hear about it being hereditary, don't you. And we've got to start thinking about things like that, yeah?'

'Mental?' Annie cringed as George did one of his over-the-top surprised faces. 'Me? Mental?' He turned to Annie, his mouth half open, obviously to ask her to back him up.

Good one, George, thought Annie. *Way to look even more mental!*

'Anyway,' Kaz waved him out of the way and snatched up her umbrella. 'Gotta go pick up some shopping for Gail. Call you, yeah?'

And with the quickest, most unconvincing hug'n'kiss Annie had seen, Kaz was out the door.

Mitchell's day hadn't got any better.

After delivering Charlie for his chemo, he'd found himself being cornered again by Mossy – complete with clipboard and a sheet of paper with 'BOWLING TEAM' written in very important capitals at the top – who had been speaking to Sarah. George had come up in the conversation as a replacement for Mitchell in the bowling; and Mossy was keen to sound Mitchell out on it.

'Never struck me as the sporty type,' Mossy said.

'Don't you think that "sport" is pushing it a bit – unless they've added it to the list for the next Olympics and haven't told anyone.'

'You'd be surprised,' Mossy said.

Mitchell didn't think he would.

'And anyway, it's about the team,' Mossy added,

clearly sensing Mitchell's scepticism. 'And,' he added with a wink, 'it's a great place to meet women.'

Like Sarah, thought Mitchell as they headed towards the cafeteria. Maybe he could get her and George off with each other. She wasn't a hundred miles away from Nina in appearance – and if Nina was George's type, maybe Sarah was. He'd ask him when he got home.

Mossy spotted someone he knew over near the window and ambled off to chat whilst Mitchell grabbed himself a coffee and a Twix. Out of the corner of his eye, he saw a movement – rhythmic, bobbing. It was a man's leg, bouncing as if in time to music. It only took Mitchell a second to recognise the man-in-black from earlier. He was slouching in a corner with a polystyrene cup and an empty sandwich packet on the table, the white cables from his mp3 player snaking into his ears. He nodded at Mitchell when he caught his eye.

Before Mitchell could launch himself on some trajectory that would keep him well away from the man, he pulled the headphones from his ears and beckoned him over.

'On your break, eh?' the man said, sitting upright as Mitchell reluctantly padded over to him.

Mitchell nodded, unsure, now he was at the man's table, whether he should actually sit down. The man answered the unspoken question on his face and gestured to the chairs opposite him.

'What you listening to?' asked Mitchell, hoping that the contents of the man's mp3 player would provide enough conversation for the duration of his coffee and

Twix. He hated it when people saw his blue scrubs and started talking about their illnesses – or, worse, the illnesses of relatives they'd come in to see. He'd never been sure whether people thought he was a surgeon, or whether they knew he was an orderly but somehow assumed that ferrying patients around the hospital caused them to absorb medical knowledge through some sort of osmosis. And his encounter with Charlie was more than enough for one day.

'You might like it,' said the man, handing the earpieces to Mitchell and fiddling with the mp3 player. With a subtle glance at them to check they weren't clogged up with alien earwax, he slipped them in.

It took him a moment to recognise it.

'That's...' Mitchell said thoughtfully, '*Sisters of Mercy*.' He narrowed his eyes and beat out the rhythm on the tabletop with his fingers. '"Alice".'

The man grinned. 'Knew you'd like it!' he said.

'Didn't say I liked it,' Mitchell replied. And then grinned back. 'It's OK.'

He started to pull the earphones out but the man raised a hand.

'One more – bet you can't get this one,' he said, dabbing at the controls.

Mitchell narrowed his eyes as sparse, doomy drums were overlaid with an equally doomy bassline. It was there, on the tip of his mind...

'Cocteau Twins!' he said decisively as the oh-so-recognisable vocals of Liz Fraser came in. 'But don't ask me what it's called.'

The man smiled and said something. Mitchell had

to pull the earphones out to hear him.

'"Alas Dies Laughing"' he repeated.

'I knew that,' Mitchell said with a look that told the man he'd not had a clue. 'Did anyone know what their songs were called?'

'I reckon they just made the titles up to sound cool – Leo, by the way.' The man extended a pale, pudgy hand and Mitchell shook it.

'Mitchell,' he said.

'So you're an expert on '80s stuff, are you?' Leo asked.

'A classic era,' Mitchell said, tearing off the end of his Twix wrapper.

'You don't look old enough,' Leo said – and Mitchell felt something tighten up inside him. *Damn!* No matter how many times it happened, he always forgot: he had the memories of an old man but the face of someone in their late 20s. Leo, however, looked every inch the kind of man whose musical era was the 1980s: a little bit gone-to-seed, in his forties. He'd probably been quite distinguished once, thought Mitchell. For a moment, he had an all-too rare flash of gratitude for his own condition. Yeah, he could overeat, put on a bit of weight. But he'd never get the grey, never feel the wearying pull of gravity dragging his mind and body down. As far as everyone else was concerned, how he looked now was how he'd look in a decade, in a century…

Mitchell blinked. Leo was saying something.

'Sorry?'

'Too right,' Leo said, tapping the mp3 player. 'Don't

make 'em like that any more. You into all that stuff, then?'

Mitchell shrugged with his face. 'Very Catholic tastes,' he said, taking a swig of his coffee.

'That's one thing that they've improved, at least,' Leo said, indicating the cup. 'Might be shit now, but it was shitter back then.'

Mitchell grinned.

'So how long you been working here then?'

'Too long.'

'Good job?'

'I've had worse. They tend to leave you alone. No one peering over your shoulder all the time.'

'What d'you do before this, then?'

Mitchell looked at Leo. What was with all the questions? Maybe the guy was just being polite. He was in a hospital, after all – maybe he just wanted to chat to someone. Mitchell had noticed that the hospital did that to people – brought out their vulnerabilities, their insecurities, their chattiness. Sometimes it was good. Sometimes it was just bloody annoying.

'Oh, this and that. What about you, then? You here visiting, or…' Mitchell switched the conversation round – he was never comfortable talking about himself, particularly about his past.

Leo rolled his eyes. 'Tests,' he said simply. 'Think it might be The Big C,' he added without a hint of self-pity.

'Sorry.'

'Don't be. No one's fault – well, if you want to blame anyone, blame you lot.'

'Us?'

Leo laughed. 'Not you personally – doctors, scientists. Keep coming up with new ways for us to get old and get new diseases, don't they? We weren't meant to live this long, I reckon.'

'I thought we were allowed three score years and ten?'

'Ha! Not even that long. I reckon evolution made us to fizzle out when we got to the big four-oh. Anything beyond that is…'

'Luck?' suggested Mitchell.

'A curse!' said Leo. There was an odd look in his eyes, like he was somewhere else.

'How old *are* you, anyway?'

'46,' Leo said, suddenly snapping back into the moment.

For one second, Mitchell wanted to tell him how *young* that was, how barely out of nappies it seemed. From his perspective, anyone under 100 was still a child. Sometimes it made him feel smart and powerful; sometimes it made him sad; and sometimes it just made him feel alien. He'd had moments, late at night, standing up on the hill, or in the car park, when he and George had been chasing Daisy and Ivan, watching the city, that the whole of humanity seemed like an anthill at his feet. But that had been *then*. That way madness lay. He couldn't afford to let his thinking take him down that route. That was how Herrick had started – thinking himself better than humanity. One moment you're a shepherd looking down at your flock – and the next you're the wolf…

'That's not old,' he said.

Leo tipped his head back and laughed again. 'Cheers, mate! But there's a lot that would think it's over the hill. Most of the unmarried birds, at any rate. Nah, not that old I s'pose – but once you get into your forties you're on the home run, aren't you? Mother Nature didn't intend us to live this long.' He waved a hand, vaguely. 'All this technology, medicine – keeping us alive longer than we've any right to be. Like moles.'

'Moles?'

'Stamp on one mole hill and it just pops up again somewhere else. Beat heart disease and strokes and you'll get got by Alzheimer's or cancer or something. Swings and roundabouts.'

'Got a point,' Mitchell agreed. 'But 46 is nothing. Still in the prime of your life. Where is it, then – if you don't mind my asking?'

Leo slapped his hand to his belly and wobbled it.

'They're not sure yet – think it's the pancreas but I'm having tests.'

'Sorry to hear it,' Mitchell said. 'But you seem pretty sorted about it. Most people wouldn't be coping as well as you.'

Leo shrugged. 'Nowt you can do, really, is there.' And then he winked. 'Just gotta take it on the chin.' He grabbed his belly again. 'Or the guts.'

'Dunno how I'd cope if I were in your position,' Mitchell said. *More than you'll ever know.* 'You're the second bloke I've spoken to today with… cancer.' He'd hesitated slightly. Some people with it didn't like the flat, in-your-faceness of the word; other people were the opposite and couldn't bear the euphemisms. Leo had already said 'The Big C', and Mitchell hoped he wasn't going to upset him. But Leo seemed fine.

'Lot of us about. Who was the other guy?'

Mitchell shook his head. 'Just a patient. Sorry, that sounded a bit callous.'

Leo smiled. 'Nah – it's true. You must see a hundred people a day. And probably don't see half of 'em again. That's what they are, patients. How was he?'

'Not good.' Mitchell paused, remembering Charlie. 'His daughter had just got pregnant, and he was worried he wouldn't live to see his grandchild.'

'That's shit, isn't it?' Leo's voice went low. 'Still, at least that's not summat I have to worry about. Neither of us was fussed with kids, really.'

'They say that attitude is halfway to beating it. You should have no trouble. You live round here?'

Leo shook his head. 'Can't you tell? Bradford. Moved down a few months back. Me and the missus split up a year and a bit back. Managed to keep it civil – until she met another bloke. Best of luck to him! And then I got made redundant and thought, "There's nowt keeping me here. No kids, no job – even the bloody dog ran off when I moved out!" So…' He tailed off and shrugged.

'And what you doing down here, workwise?'

'Bit of bar work, shop work – anything going really. This bugger –' he gestured to his belly '– has put paid to anything more exciting.'

'Well,' said Mitchell, not quite sure why he was offering, 'if I hear of anything…'

'Cheers, Mitchell, that's good of you. Hang on.' Leo

dug in his pocket for a bit of paper – but couldn't find a pen. Mitchell didn't have one either.

'Hang on,' said Mitchell and nipped over to where Mossy was clearly trying to recruit someone else to his Army of Darkness. He deftly reached over his shoulder and swiped the one from Mossy's clipboard.

'Oi!' said Mossy.

'You'll get it back in a second.'

Mossy kept his eye on the pen as Mitchell returned to Leo and let him scribble his mobile number on the bit of paper.

'Don't worry if nothing comes up,' Leo said, handing back the pen. 'But cheers anyway.' He glanced at his watch. 'Right! Best be off.'

He gathered up his mp3 player and began to put it in his pocket, and then stopped.

'Look,' he said. 'Sorry if this sounds a bit daft or forward or summat, but what you doing tomorrow night?'

'Um,' said Mitchell, suddenly thrown.

'Not chattin' you up or owt,' Leo grinned, 'just that Bite Me! are doing a gig at the uni.'

'*Bite Me!*?'

It took a couple of seconds for the name to register.

'They're still going?'

Mitchell remembered them: he'd seen them in Sheffield back in, oooh, '83 or '84. A bit fancy-dress-Goth but pretty good. They'd had a couple of singles and then vanished.

'Well, I...'

Leo raised a hand. 'No probs, mate – sorry. Daft idea,

asking someone you've only just met if they want to go to a gig.' He laughed awkwardly. 'I could be a total nutter for all you know.'

'No, it's OK,' Mitchell said. 'I think I'm busy, anyway, but thanks for the offer.'

'Cool, mate.' There was a sudden awkwardness as Leo finished pocketing his mp3 player and extricated himself from his corner.

Mitchell stood up and tossed back the last of his coffee, accepting Leo's handshake. 'Have a good night, anyway,' he said.

'Yeah. Take care of yourself, Mitchell.'

With a matey wink, Leo left the cafeteria.

Mitchell watched him go. He felt curiously edgy, although he couldn't put his finger on why. He was pretty sure it wasn't the cancer – he came across dozens of people with terminal (or potentially terminal) illnesses every week. He gathered up the litter from the table and took it over to the bin on his way out. Maybe it was the mention of the '80s – not a particularly good time for Mitchell. He'd fallen in with a crowd of vampires that had pushed him to the edge of – and, on a couple of occasions, beyond – what he thought he was capable of, and it wasn't a part of his history he was keen to revisit.

But no, that wasn't it either.

Over the years, Mitchell had learned to trust his instincts, even if he often ignored what they screamed at him. A century of living amongst humans, scenting their emotions, tuning in to their hopes and, more often, their fears had left him with what he thought of as an insight into their minds.

But with Leo...

Mitchell shook his head, tipped the rubbish into the bin, and went back to work.

It was at times like this that Annie realised quite how alone she was.

When George and Mitchell were at home, when there were other people in the house – God, even when Gemma had been around – she didn't feel so bad. If there had been some consistency to her life, she felt she'd have something to work with. But one minute she was invisible to everyone except George and Mitchell, and the next, complete strangers could see her. That hadn't happened for a while now, and Annie had contemplated starting a diary, trying to find some rhyme or reason to her ghostiness. At one point, she'd thought she had it nailed: when she was feeling uptight or angry, no one could see her; and when she was calm and settled and happy, they could. But until Kaz's visit earlier on, she'd been feeling quite good, despite the business with Gemma. Maybe that was it – maybe her ghost-hormones were still up in the air. Maybe just the presence of Kaz had wound her up so much that she'd faded out. And it wasn't even as if *she* could tell – it was only from other people's reactions that she knew whether she was visible or not.

It was like PMT, only she couldn't mark it on a calendar. Why weren't there any books or websites on this sort of thing? *The Dummy's Guide To Being Dead*. She'd pay good money for a copy of that. In many ways, she and George were alike – and different to Mitchell. She and George didn't have any kind of support network. Apart from Tully, George didn't know any other werewolves that he could chat things over with, and she didn't know any other dead people – not any more. Was that a good thing? Maybe that's what she needed – a ghost friend: someone to sit down and chat with and laugh and cry about stuff. Have poltergeisting competitions, go a-haunting, work out the rules of their new lives. Deaths.

Maybe she should hang out in graveyards. No, from her own experience ghosts didn't haunt the places where they were buried; only the ones where they died. Maybe she should ask Mitchell or George if they ever had a 'Bring a recently deceased friend to work' day. The idea of graveyards made her think of Gilbert, the fellow ghost she'd met not so long ago. He'd shown her her own grave.

Annie stared listlessly at the third cup of tea she'd made since George had stormed out, accusing her of being prejudiced against Kaz and Gail. Well, she thought, 'stormed out' might be a bit of an exaggeration: he'd glared at her, taken a deep breath, grabbed his keys and buggered off. And then come back for his coat. For George, she supposed, that *was* 'storming out'.

It was only when she suddenly found herself missing Gilbert that she realised she needed to pull herself together. George was a grown man, he could make his own decisions. And it's not like anyone would be getting hurt. Well… she wouldn't put money on Kaz being a particularly benign influence on George's life.

Maybe it'd actually be good for him.

Yes, she thought. Think positive!

Chapter
THREE

'I think it's a bloody *mad* idea!' shouted Mitchell, storming through into the lounge. He whirled round. 'George? With a kid?' He glared at Annie who was still in the kitchen, wincing.

She realised she was fiddling with her neck. 'Calm down, Mitchell,' she said.

'Calm down? Have either of you thought this through?'

'It's early days,' Annie tried to placate him. 'They haven't done much more than agree that it's going to happen. Mitchell, this could be the best thing to happen to George since Nina. Well, since...'

Mitchell leaned forwards and ran his hands through his hair.

Annie came and sat on the sofa next to him.

'It's only a kid,' she said gently. 'It's not like he told

her about the werewolf stuff, is it?'

Mitchell turned his head slowly to look at her, his hair slipping through his fingers.

'And you know, do you,' he asked steadily, 'for a fact, that George's condition isn't hereditary?'

Annie opened her mouth to say 'Of course it isn't – he was scratched by a werewolf, not given birth to by one.' And then closed it again, as she realised that no, she didn't know – *for a fact* – that it wasn't hereditary; George's condition was almost as much of a guessing game as hers was.

'You reckon...' she said slowly.

Mitchell sat up straight. 'No, I don't reckon. I... I don't *know*. That's the whole point. Yes, werewolves are... created, made, whatever, when they're scratched by another one. But *who knows* about this stuff, hmm? Maybe there are hundreds of werewolves running around whose mothers or fathers were werewolves too.'

'No,' said Annie firmly. 'That doesn't make sense – wouldn't the world be overrun with them by now? Once a month there'd be thousands and thousands of unexplained killings all over the world.'

'Why?' Mitchell asked simply. 'As far as we know, George isn't going to live for ever. Not like me. And how many other werewolves has he created so far?'

Annie shrugged.

'Exactly – it might be one – it might be ten. But think about it: he could have fathered as many *kids* in that time – more. People do, but they don't go on to overrun the world with their grandkids, do they? Cos they die eventually.' He stopped and held her gaze. 'It's not werewolves that are capable of overwhelming the rest of you through sheer numbers. It's us you've got to watch out for with that.'

Annie wasn't sure whether that had been a joke or not.

'So it *could* be hereditary… I hadn't thought about that.'

There was an awkward silence.

'Wouldn't it have showed up in some tests or something? He *has* been in hospital before, hasn't he?'

Mitchell nodded. 'But if it's a virus, maybe – or something genetic – there's hardly going to be a little hairy bug in his bloodstream with a T-shirt on saying *I'm a Werewolf*, is there?' He rubbed his lower lip with his thumbnail. 'We've got to talk him out of it, Annie.'

'Whoa,' said Annie, raising her hands. 'What's with the "we"? I already told him it might not be a very good idea earlier, I don't think he's going to want to listen to anything *I* say.'

'Fine,' said Mitchell, glaring at her. 'I'll do it, then.'

'I'm not saying I don't agree with you – but you've known him longer and you're a man and…' She flapped her hands vaguely. 'He just might listen more if it came from you, that's all I'm saying.'

'Yeah,' said Mitchell after a moment. 'You could be right. Maybe it's just me.'

'Bad day?'

He pulled a face. 'Not so much bad as…' He searched around for the word. 'Unsettling. I can't put my finger on it, but…' He gave a mock shudder, like a dog shaking off raindrops. 'That kinda thing – you know?'

Annie nodded. She knew.

It felt like he'd opened the wrong door and stumbled into the headmaster's office.

Mitchell was sitting in the armchair, facing the door. Annie was nowhere to be seen.

'Good day?' he asked brightly, knowing full well what this was about.

'I've had better. Listen, George—'

George spun round from hanging his coat up, his palm raised. 'If it's about me and Kaz and Gail and the baby—'

'"*And the baby*"?' said Mitchell. 'George, listen to yourself. It's not been a day and already you're talking about it like it's something real.'

George waggled his still-raised hand. 'What part of this don't you understand? I thought it was a fairly universal gesture of "Stop!". Good job you don't drive, really, isn't it, otherwise God knows how many people you'd have mown down by now?'

'You're not list—'

George brought the other hand up to join the first and waggled the two of them at Mitchell, palms front. 'And you're not *looking*, Mitchell. Now, please, can we drop this conversation otherwise it's going to be a very tense evening in here.'

He raised his eyebrows and stared at Mitchell until he finally nodded.

'Good – where's Annie?'

Mitchell gestured with his head. 'Upstairs. Keeping out of the way.'

George shook his head as he went to make a cuppa and check what was in the fridge for tea.

'So,' he called back to Mitchell. 'You said you'd had better.'

'Better what?'

'Better days at work. What happened?'

'I've signed you up for the bowling team,' Mitchell answered brightly after a second.

'You've what?'

'Well…' Mitchell was trying his best grin. 'I thought you needed a bit of exercise – and it's a great way to meet women.'

'If you mean Phyllis and Barbara, I *am* going to have to kill you, you know.'

Mitchell laughed – and the little knot of tightness that had been building up inside George since he'd got home relaxed and fizzled away. Back to normal.

'I mean women at the bowling alley, not on Mossy's team.'

'Have you actually *been* bowling? It's full of couples and groups of couples and sad, lonely people hoping they'll meet someone at a bowling alley. Well, guess what – I'm neither! Fish fingers or chicken kievs?'

'Fish fingers. And no it's not… OK, even if it *is*, stands to reason that some of them won't be complete mingers, doesn't it? All they want is to get their hands on a few nice balls…'

'Even by your standards, that was a bit crude, wasn't it?'

Annie was standing at the foot of the stairs, arms folded, throwing Mitchell an icy look. Presumably, thought George, as he shook the last of the oven chips onto a baking tray, pissed off at Mitchell for not having read the riot act about the baby.

His baby.

The hairs on George's arms suddenly stood up. He stared at them, fascinated, and was on the point of showing Annie – but stopped himself. They wouldn't understand and would only start on the 'Have you thought this thing through?' again.

This wasn't theirs. This was *his*. He wasn't going to let them spoil it.

Annie thawed before the fish fingers did.

She couldn't be too annoyed at Mitchell – after all, she'd been the one who'd said he should tackle George on his own. She'd heard the conversation the two of them had had from the top of the stairs. And whilst she agreed with Mitchell that, without knowing the real nature of George's wolfiness, it was a silly idea for him to go fathering kids all over the place, part of her couldn't help but see it as a good thing. For George, at least.

She and Owen had talked about kids – partly in that jokey way that you do, when you're still in the first few months of a relationship and don't want to jinx things; and partly in a 'testing out the other person' sort of way. The fact that neither of them had raised an eyebrow at talk of turning one of the bedrooms into a nursery had seemed like a good sign. Maybe that was why she was reacting the way she was to the George and Gail thing: jealousy. But that was one door that she wanted to keep closed. For now. And as she watched George faff about in the kitchen, she wondered whether Mitchell's reaction to George's potential fatherhood wasn't bound up more in his own situation than she'd realised too. Annie had no idea whether Mitchell harboured any secret desires to be a father – it wasn't something they'd ever discussed. But his reaction to George's announcement would make sense if he, too, had worries about his own condition. Did he, secretly, wonder if it were transmissible by sex? The fact that it was obviously connected with blood made it seem more likely that it was some sort of nasty in his bloodstream: and how would a vampire go about having sex – baby-making sex – without risking exposing his or her partner to that nasty? Did Mitchell always use condoms, just in case? Annie realised her mind was going places that it really shouldn't.

They plonked themselves in front of the telly with their fish fingers and chips (and peas!) and watched a documentary about eels.

Occasionally, Annie could see Mitchell giving her glances – his eyes flicking to George, momentarily. Yes, it was still the elephant in the room. But for now, it was a well-behaved elephant, wearing a couple of scatter cushions and doing a good impersonation of an armchair.

When George got up to go to the loo, she and Mitchell looked at each other.

'This can't go on,' Mitchell said.

'It's his decision.'

'Maybe he's not even thought about whether he can pass it on to someone else,' he whispered, glancing towards the door to the stairs. 'If he hasn't, don't we owe it to him to say something? Not to mention to Gail and Kaz.'

'Yeah,' said Annie, without much enthusiasm. 'To Gail and Kaz. But...' She nodded. 'Yeah.'

Mitchell nodded in agreement.

'Yeah... but...'

'Yeah but,' mocked a voice from just out of sight. George's head appeared around the staircase door. His voice was clipped and strained. 'You're not the only one who can listen in on conversations, you know.'

Annie glanced at Mitchell.

'But *have* you thought about it?'

'About what?' spat George with an intensity that frightened Annie. 'About whether this... this...' He gestured angrily at himself. 'This *thing* can be passed on to someone else by shagging them? Of course I've thought about it. I've thought about nothing else all day!' He glared at Mitchell and then back at Annie, and pursed his lips together. And he was talking in that particular way he had, emphasising the 't's at the ends of words. Controlled. Precise. Like he was holding himself back. Was this what it was like for him when he felt himself *changing*?

'Or d'you two think I'm the kind of person who actually *enjoys* going round giving people sexually transmitted diseases? "Oh! I wonder who I should infect tonight!"'

'That's not what we—' began Mitchell, but George was on a roll, striding into the lounge.

'Maybe I'm so messed up about my own condition that I have to go spreading it around – "share the love". That what you think of me? Is that what you think I did to Nina? Well, good. I'm glad that's out in the open. Now, if you'll excuse me, I'm going to go to my room to think about what a selfish, evil person I am.' He paused and looked at the two of them expectantly. 'If that's OK with you two.'

Mitchell and Annie looked at each other.

When they looked back, George had gone.

20 June 1987
IBIZA

Now this is more like it! This is a real holiday – sun, sea and (ex)sanguination!

I know, I know, but it was too good a joke to miss, wasn't it?

Oh well, suit yerselves, as Frankie Howerd says.

Can you tell I'm a little bit drunk. Only a bit, mind – alcohol doesn't hit us quite as hard as it does them. Gin's pretty good, for some reason. Discovered that from a friend of mine, Baxter. He's dead now. But he didn't half taste good. Our bodies are too good at mopping up the broken, drunk bits and repairing them. Has its downsides, obviously – takes an awful lot to get one of us pissed. We're not cheap dates. On the upside, of course, it's always good to be in control. But sod it, I'm on holiday in the hedonism capital of Europe. If I can't get a bit pissed here, where can I?

I shouldn't have been surprised at the number of us here

– but I am. Makes sense, really – a constant flow of people, in and out, sleeping around. People who might go missing for days before anyone realises something's wrong. And the local policia *– well, they're overstretched as it is. What with all the drugs and the drink, there's always a fight or two down in San Antonio to keep them busy. And if a body or two washes up on the shore, after the fishes and crabs have had their way with them for a while, well, who's to say they didn't just get drunk and fall in the sea, staggering back to their apartment late at night?*

Obviously, I was joking about the sun earlier. Our Mediterranean cousins – and the black ones, of course – don't fare much better. You'd think they might, wouldn't you? Sunhats and staying indoors until teatime. Not that that arouses much suspicion here, either: only the stupid tourists spend much time out in the day, and they're not the ones I'd choose anyway. I prefer the night owls, like myself. Something just a bit more sophisticated, you know what I mean?

That's why I prefer Ibiza Old Town. Just a bit classier than the other resorts that are springing up like concrete barracks to house the sheep. I've found myself a nice, quiet little bar. Glass of red wine. Cigarette.

And a beautiful woman.

Like the one last night.

Yes, another beautiful woman. Hell, why not? I'm on holiday, after all.

Ah, she's giving me the come-on. Makes a change. Makes it feel almost normal – less like a predator moving in on his prey. It's good to keep things fresh, don't you think?

She's been sitting there for twenty minutes, drinking

vodka and coke or something, smoking cheap Spanish cigarettes. She's not checked her watch once, so either she's on her own for the evening, or she's being very cool about waiting. I reckon it's the former. Easier for me. The one last night was in some club in San Antonio – she was with a group of girlfriends, all leery and pissed. The novelty wore off pretty quickly so I cut to the chase, as it were, and took her outside. Told her she had beautiful legs and feet. Admired her shoes. Bit her on the ankle. Took a bit of doing, keeping her quiet while I drained her, but in a weird way I think it turned her on a bit. Well, until she passed out. Keeps the authorities on their toes, biting them in strange places. And I don't mean around the back of the bar.

But I think I'll be a bit more traditional with this little beauty. We'll see.

'Hi,' I say, leaning across and extending a hand. 'My name's Mitchell. That's a beautiful necklace...'

Chapter
FOUR

'Babes,' said Gail, wafting the smoke from Kaz's cigarette away from her face. 'You're really going to have to stop that.'

'What?' She looked at the cigarette. 'This? This is *medicinal*. It's ethically grown and harvested, and half the profits go to women's—'

'Says who?'

Kaz pulled an *isn't it obvious?* face. 'Moonpaw, of course. She says it'll help generate a positive energy aura for our little girl.'

'And that's another thing…'

They were sitting outside Starbucks, drinking coffee under a sky trying its bloody hardest to rain but only managing a half-hearted drizzle. Since Kaz had started getting pally with that mad old hippy Moonpaw ('Moonpaw', for God's sake!), Gail reckoned she was completely losing it. Every time Kaz came home she was spouting even more New Age bollocks. First it had been crystals and dreamcatchers and chakras – they'd been innocuous enough. But when she came home with a plastic baggie of Moonpaw's vile 'cleansing roll-up mixture', Gail had put her foot down good and firm, and had insisted: no more smoking indoors. As winter drew on, Gail hoped that the novelty would soon wear off. She didn't fancy the idea of having to sit shivering outside cafes and pubs for the rest of her life.

'There's a long tradition of boys in my family,' Gail said. 'I'm the first girl in three generations, so don't go getting your hopes up too much.'

'And that,' said Kaz brightly, 'is why Moonpaw and Rainbow want us round for tea at the weekend, so's Moonpaw can help.'

'Help? What d'you mean, help?'

'She's going to do some… some rituals. Ancient Arabic, yeah?' There was a vagueness to her tone that didn't bode well. 'They'll help realign the energy fields in your ovaries…'

'Whoa there!' said Gail. 'That lunatic bint is going nowhere *near* my ovaries. My energy fields are perfectly aligned as they are, thanks very much.'

'No, serious – like, she can do this thing and it'll *guarantee* that it's a girl.'

'And she'd put money on it, would she?'

'You're telling me you don't want our child – our *special* child – to be a girl?'

Gail patted Kaz on the knee. 'Our child *will* be

special, babes, no matter whether it's a boy, a girl or a puppy.' She paused. 'Although thinking about it – a puppy would be kinda nice.'

Kaz's face dropped into a sulky pout. 'You're not taking this seriously, Gail.'

'Excuse me? Energy fields around my ovaries? Cleansing tobacco? I think serious is waving at us from the end of the runway. Besides, it's my body. I get to say what's done to it.'

'We've been over this,' said Kaz, her voice now an irritating wheedle. 'I'd have the baby if I could, but my mother said that I've got a very narrow pelvis.'

'And how would *she* know?'

'I've told you, I nearly got caught in some railings when I was little, yeah, and the only reason I got out was because I had this, like, narrow pelvis.' Kaz gestured to her hips. 'It's in my medical records and everything.'

Gail raised a sceptical eyebrow.

'Besides,' Kaz added, flicking her cigarette out into the street where it almost landed in a passing baby buggy, 'you're so much more...' She looked Gail up and down and made curvaceous gestures with her hands.

'Careful...' warned Gail.

'Motherly.'

'Hmmm...'

Kaz suddenly jumped up and started waving. 'George! George!'

George spotted them and came trotting over.

There was, Gail thought, something adorable about

George. That was the word: *adorable*. Although – unlike Kaz – she had the tact to recognise that it might not be the kind of word he'd want to be described with. Like an eager puppy. Good natured.

God, thought Gail as George gave them both a hug. *I am having a puppy!*

'Sorry about this,' Gail said, gesturing to the sky and the faint drizzle that had started. 'Only her ladyship here insisted on being able to smoke.'

George grinned sympathetically. 'Um, coffee?' he asked.

'Oh yeah, I'll have a big, erm, creamy one – with all the trimmings,' Kaz jumped in. 'And a low-fat one for Gail.'

Gail smiled tightly. 'Yeah – with nothing in it at all. And hold the water.' George looked a bit thrown. 'Oh, go on then – a big skinny latte, please.'

'Thought you were on the fruit teas, anyway?' George gestured at Kaz's half-empty cup.

'I was until I drank that muck at yours – what was in it? Ribena?'

George smiled awkwardly and went inside.

Gail leaned forwards. 'Look, seriously, Kaz – you are sure about this, aren't you?'

'Course I am.' Kaz pulled a face. 'Why?'

'Because this – much as you, in your good-natured way, probably think differently – isn't just about you. It's not even just about us. It's about George, too. We're asking him to do probably the biggest thing in his life.'

Kaz stared at her, and suddenly – in a gesture so

comic that Gail almost laughed – threw both hands up to her mouth.

'Oh my God!' she said, eyes wide. 'You're having second thoughts, aren't you? Oh my God!'

'How many times…' said Gail through gritted teeth, trying not to lose her temper. 'No, babes, I am not having second thoughts. It was me who brought up the idea of our having a baby in the first place, yeah? And it was me who suggested that I carry it, yeah?' She grabbed Kaz's hands and held them tight – more to stop her doing any more diva theatrics with them than anything else. 'This is going to be our baby and I want it one hundred per cent. But I want to be sure that George wants it one hundred per cent too.'

'Why?' said Kaz, suddenly brittle. 'He's not going to be bringing it up, is he?'

'That's what we're all here to talk about, isn't it?' Gail put on her most reasonable face and looked Kaz right in the eyes until she eventually nodded. Only then did Gail let go of her hands. Just in time for George to arrive.

'That's…' he opened the lid of one of the coffees, 'yours – and that's yours.'

He huddled in between them.

'Right,' he said brightly, raising his cup. 'To babies!'

George quite liked Gail.

Not in a sexual way, really (although he did think she had a lovely skin colour – like milky coffee, not far off Annie's own – and gorgeous hazel eyes. And quite nice breasts. And her arse was one of those sensual, bouncy ones… *Stop it, George!*). Just in a 'really nice, down-to-earth, sound and sorted person' sort of way. Quite why she'd hooked up with a fruitcake like Kaz he wasn't sure – but then there was no accounting for taste, was there?

Since Kaz had dropped the bombshell the day before, he'd found himself unable to think about anything else. And, despite what Annie and Mitchell seemed to think, the possibility of Gail giving birth, in nine months' time (give or take) to a hairy little thing with claws and fangs had been quite high up on the list.

But, just for now, just for an hour, he wanted to think about it in as normal a way as possible. Well, as normal a way as you *could* think about a baby created by werewolf sperm donated to two slightly mad lesbians.

Yes, just an hour or so of normal baby stuff.

'How's Mitchell about it?' Gail asked him.

And straight out of the window with the normal.

'I think he might take a bit of time to come round.'

Gail threw Kaz a sharp look.

'Kaz said he was fine about it.'

'Oh, he is,' George flustered. 'He will be.'

'This isn't about Mitchell,' cut in Kaz. 'This is, like, about *us*, yeah?'

Gail ignored Kaz, and George found himself remembering why he liked her.

'Babes,' she said, 'Mitchell is George's family and his friend. It's George's decision – and ours – but it's got to be right for everyone.'

'Look, about this "Mitchell is George's family" thing,' began George. 'I don't know what Kaz has been saying – but me and Mitchell… we really *are* just friends.'

Kaz raised a knowing eyebrow. Gail just nodded.

'It's OK – I know. Kaz does tend to get a bit… carried away.'

'I so do not!' Kaz said indignantly.

'The woman in the butcher's?' Gail reminded her.

Kaz suddenly looked very sheepish.

'What happened with the woman in the butcher's?' George was eager to know.

'Gail!' warned Kaz.

'Suffice to say, it's the main reason Kaz decided to go veggie.'

'I was a veggie *before* that. And anyway, how else d'you explain the extra sausages she used to slip in, eh?'

'You were a veggie and shopping at the butcher's?' George was losing track.

'For the dog,' Kaz said pointedly. 'Dogs have to eat meat.'

'Isn't that cats?'

Gail raised her hands in an *I told you!* gesture.

'Anyway,' said Kaz, 'it died.'

'D'uh!' said George. 'And you're planning on bringing up a *baby*…?'

'A baby's different,' said Kaz primly.

'Yeah,' agreed George. 'You can't just put bowls of food and a lot of newspaper down when you go away for the weekend.'

'That little girl –' Kaz caught Gail's eye '– or boy is going to be the best brought up little girl – or boy – in the whole wide world, right? She's going to have, like, the bestest mummies in the world.'

'And daddy,' added Gail.

'Course,' agreed Kaz. She reached up and squeezed his cheek. 'George is going to be the bestest part-time dad in the world, too!'

'You know what's the worst thing?'

'Mmmm?' Mitchell looked up from the telly to see Annie coming in with two more cups of coffee.

'The worst thing – about this baby.'

'Apart from the fact that it could be some hideous mutant hybrid, you mean?'

'Apart from that.' She plonked them on the table. 'It's the fact that we can't do any "litters of puppies" jokes.'

Mitchell just stared at her, eyes wide – before a huge grin cracked his face. 'If George even *thought* you were thinking of jokes like that…'

'Yeah…' Annie stared at the cups for a few seconds, before looking up. 'He'd set the baby on me!'

The two of them collapsed in howls of laughter, that only ended when Mitchell knocked over his cuppa and ran to kitchen to get a cloth.

'We wouldn't have to wipe up, though,' Annie said, still convulsed. 'We could just point to the spill and the baby'd do the rest.'

'No more washing up,' Mitchell added, wiping the tears from his eyes. 'Just leave the plates on the floor.'

'We'd have to get a sign for the door: BEWARE OF THE BABY.'

Mitchell screwed up the cloth he'd been wiping the floor with and threw it at Annie, hitting her square in the face. She squealed, half in outrage, half in laughter, as the phone rang.

'Hello,' said Mitchell, trying to catch his breath as he snatched it up. 'Oh. Hi George.'

Annie busied herself making another cuppa – because, obviously, the one she'd made a few minutes ago would be going cold.

Mitchell put down the phone and walked back into the kitchen just as she waved her hand above the kettle and it clicked off.

'Did you do that?' he asked admiringly.

'What?'

'Turn the kettle off?' He wiggled his fingers like a bad stage magician.

'Nah. You never done that?'

'Use my psychic powers to turn off domestic appliances?' He shook his head. 'Not as often as you might think.'

'No – *pretend* you could –' she wiggled her fingers, spookily, again '– and then get a bit excited if you got the timing right?'

Mitchell gave her a look.

'Just me, then?'

'Just you. That was George.'

'I guessed. How is he?'

'He seems fine – he's having coffee with Gail and

Kaz. They're probably going through baby name books.'

'Fido,' suggested Annie, spooning coffee into two mugs. 'Or Scooby.' Her eyes lit up. 'Scooby! That would be a cool name.'

'Less so if it's a girl.'

'Lassie?'

'Hmmmm.' Mitchell wasn't convinced.

'What did he want?'

'He wants us all to have a night out together.'

'When?'

'He suggested tonight.' Mitchell suddenly pulled a thoughtful face and dug around in his pocket. He pulled out a crumpled bit of paper.

'What's that?'

'A guy I met yesterday – at the hospital. Leo. There's a gig at the uni that he thought I might be up for – ever heard of Bite Me!'

'*Bite Me!*? You're sure he didn't just *say* "Bite me!"?' Annie made a chomping face.

'They were big in the '80s.'

'So was Margaret Thatcher, but you wouldn't get me going to one of her gigs. Not unless it's that "dancing on her grave" party that everyone's planning. What's wrong with just going to the pub?'

'You really fancy sitting around a table whilst they go on about baby clothes and what school they need to get it into? Besides, Kaz'll be smoking those things of hers and will insist that we sit outside with her, freezing our bollocks off, so she's not on her own. Harder to do at a gig.'

'You've got a point. Who's this Leo, then?'

'Just a patient. Seemed OK. Maybe cancer.'

'You asked his star sign? Thought he was Leo, anyway.'

Mitchell gave her a Paddington Bear stare.

'Oh,' she said as the penny suddenly dropped. 'God. Right.' She poured milk into the mugs. 'It'll make a change, I s'pose.'

Mitchell reached for the phone. 'And if all else fails, we can just trip Kaz up and watch her get trampled to death by the crowd.'

'I'll get my boots,' grinned Annie.

Three frappucappumochachocolatas later and George was feeling decidedly buzzy. In fact the last time he'd been this buzzy had been when he'd been given some Pro Plus years ago, during his exams. He'd spent the rest of the night bouncing off the walls – until someone pointed out that they had actually been echinacea tablets.

The drizzle had turned to half-arsed sunshine and Kaz's ciggies had stopped bothering him. Even Mitchell had seemed surprisingly up about the whole gang of them having a night out together.

'Have you thought about where you're going to have it?' he asked Gail.

'Like, at home, obviously,' jumped in Kaz, as if the thought of having it in a hospital were equivalent to saying 'Between two slices of bread, medium rare'.

'We thought a home birth would be nice,' agreed Gail.

'Oh!' said Kaz suddenly, pulling a pen and rainbow-covered notepad out of her bag. 'Poundstretcher!'

'Classy,' muttered George.

'They've got paddling pools for a pound,' she said, scribbling furiously.

'Isn't it going to be a bit young for that?' George asked.

'For the birth, dummy.'

'For a pound?' said Gail. 'You have noticed that I'm not exactly a size zero, haven't you? Not sure you get much paddling pool for a pound, babes.'

'You might be right.' Kaz pursed her lips. 'We'll get two.'

'One for each breast,' said George, still high on the caffeine – before he saw their faces. 'I said that out loud, didn't I?'

Gail grinned. Kaz just scowled. George was pleased it was Gail who was going to be the mother and not Kaz: the thought of having to negotiate all this with her was a scary one. Although it seemed that Kaz was appropriating this birth for herself anyway.

'And what about names?'

Kaz suddenly began flicking through her notepad, her face lit up with excitement. Gail pulled a sympathetic face at George.

'You've heard of numerology, yeah?' said Kaz, settling in for the long haul. 'Well, I've got this book at home…'

Mitchell was surprised to see quite so many people queuing for tickets. Bite Me! hadn't been that big way back when, and he found it hard to believe that doing the uni circuit ever since could have got them that many new fans. Maybe they'd been 'big in Europe' – which usually meant 'Germany'. He was less surprised to see quite how annoying and loud students were, though. Some things never changed. A bit like Mitchell himself.

Annie was hanging around outside.

'I should go out with dead people more often,' Mitchell quipped.

'Why?'

'Cheap dates.' Mitchell held up a single ticket. 'You still invisible, then?'

Annie nodded. 'No one's tried chatting me up so far.'

'And that's down to your invisibility?'

Annie hit him on the arm.

'Ouch – for a dead girl, you certainly pack a punch – oh, there's Leo!'

He waved and Leo came over.

'All right, mate,' Leo said.

'Yeah, good,' said Mitchell. 'I didn't get you a ticket – just in case, you know, you couldn't make it at the last minute.'

Leo nodded. He looked much as he had done the day before, only with a dark red shirt and no silver wing-tips. It was already dark and the light from the concourse's sodium lights made him look oddly paler than he'd done before. For a moment, Mitchell wondered if he were wearing make-up. Maybe it was the whole goth thing.

'George and the others'll be here soon,' Mitchell said. 'Whatcha been up to, then?'

Leo's eyes flicked sideways and then back to Mitchell. 'Not gonna introduce us, then?'

'What?'

'Sorry,' said Leo, looking at Annie again. *Looking at Annie.* 'You're together, aren't you?'

'Oh!' said Mitchell with what must have been a stupid look on his face. 'Yeah. Sorry, sorry – Leo, Annie; Annie, Leo.'

Mitchell caught Annie's expression – she was smiling. They shook hands, Mitchell watching closely, just to check that Leo's hand didn't simply slip through Annie's.

'Mitchell your boyfriend, then?'

'Oh God no!' said Annie sharply.

'Thanks,' whispered Mitchell.

'Housemates – sort of.'

'Sort of?'

'It's complicated,' Annie said.

'Right,' said Leo.

There was an awkward pause.

'Glad you could come, anyway,' he said eventually. 'To be honest, I didn't expect to hear from you. Probably came across a bit of a twat.' He glanced at Annie. 'No offence.'

'What?'

'Sorry – swearing around ladies. Bad habit.'

'It's OK,' Annie said, patting his arm. 'Last time I checked it was the twenty-first century, so I reckon you'll get away with it.'

'Nice one!' Leo grinned. He winked at Mitchell. 'I like her.'

Mitchell was still trying to work out whether this whole evening was plunging hellward at a rate of knots or whether Leo had managed to pull it back up by its bootlaces, when he caught sight of George, doing an awkward dance through the crowd, trying his best not to bump into anyone. Mitchell could see his lips moving as he apologised, over and over.

'All right?' asked Mitchell. He saw George's eyes. 'Bloody hell, what happened to you?'

'Caffeine happened to me. Why didn't you tell me how good it is?'

Mitchell pulled an *ouch!* face.

'Yes,' agreed George. 'I am not going to be able to sleep until February now. But on the upside – I don't care!'

He looked at Annie and gave a smile and a little wave.

'This is Leo,' said Annie. 'Mitchell's friend.'

'Nice to meet you, mate,' said Leo.

'George,' said George, managing an awkward handshake.

Suddenly he looked at Annie – and then at Mitchell.

'Um, Mitchell...' he said, grabbing his elbow. 'A word?'

Mitchell shrugged to Leo and Annie and let George guide him round the corner.

'What,' said George, his voice all clipped and controlled again, 'is Annie doing here?'

'Are the dead not allowed a night out now, then?'

'You know what I mean – Leo can obviously see her, can't he?' George was gabbling and Mitchell glanced round to see if anyone had noticed. Decaff only for George from now on.

'Yeah,' agreed Mitchell. '*That* part of the plan came as a bit of a surprise to both of us. Still, saves on those awkward conversations where only two of us can...' He tailed off and his mouth dropped open. 'Oh God!' he hissed. 'Kaz and Gail.'

George clutched at Mitchell's arm. 'Leo can see her, but what if Gail can and Kaz *can't*? Mitchell, this is going to be a disaster.'

'You were the one who brought her.'

'Yes, cos *you* were the one about to have a baby, and *you* were the one who—' Mitchell bit his tongue. 'Look, no point in arguing this now. What are we going to – Oh shit.'

George followed Mitchell's gaze – to where Gail and Kaz were making their way through the crowd towards them.

'What are we going to do?' flustered George.

'We'll handle it. It's happened before.'

'Not like this it hasn't. Out in public, with – what's his name? – Leo. And those two.' George shook his head. 'Look,' he said. 'You take those two and go inside. I'll tell Gail and Kaz you've gone to get a good place near the front or something. And then I'll try to keep them away from you when we get in.'

'Hang on, George – maybe we don't have to.'

'Of course we have to.'

'No – think about it. Leo can see her, so that means that Gail and Kaz can probably see her too.'

'That's how it works, is it?'

'Well how *does* it work, Brainiac?'

'Don't ask me – I'm not the one who thought it was a good idea to bring a ghost to a concert.'

'It's a gig, George, a gig. Not a concert.'

It was too late to escape Gail and Kaz, though. They gave Mitchell a hug and a kiss.

'Has it freaked you out, then?' grinned Gail.

For a moment, Mitchell thought she was talking about Annie, but George stepped in.

'Mitchell's really happy for us,' he said, obviously trying not to sound too pointed. 'Aren't you?'

'Yeah, yeah – brilliant.' He gave them both another hug for good measure.

'George is like, *sooo* excited,' Kaz said. 'So where is he?'

'Who?' asked Mitchell and George in unison.

'This friend of yours – the one who told you about the gig.'

'He's…'

'Over there,' said George.

'Inside,' said Mitchell.

'Over there, inside.'

George looked at Mitchell.

Kaz raised an eyebrow.

'He's stood you up, hasn't he?' she said understandingly. 'Don't worry – people are shits like that. It's, like, always happening to me.'

'Have you two got tickets?' asked Gail.

George and Mitchell looked at each other, trying to work out what the right answer was before they opened their mouths and made themselves look like tits again.

'I've got mine,' Mitchell said.

'Right,' George said too brightly. 'Let's go and get ours. See you in there.' With a slightly wild look, he escorted the two women inside as Mitchell nodded and dipped back round the corner to where Leo and Annie were chatting away quite happily.

'Where's George?' she asked.

'He's gone in to get his ticket. With Gail and Kaz.'

Leo laughed.

'The more the merrier, eh?'

'Yeah,' said Mitchell. 'The more the merrier.'

Mitchell had almost forgotten what it was like to be around so many people. So many young, vibrant, smelly, noisy people.

Since he'd gone 'on the wagon', so many people around him was the equivalent of an alcoholic taking a daytrip to a wine warehouse: all those people, all that *blood* – so close… He felt his heart racing and had to take a few moments to breathe slowly and deeply, to calm down. Only a vampire could understand how difficult it was to be in crowds. Particularly crowds of young people. *Jesus!*, thought Mitchell. *I feel like some sort of pervert.* It was as though everyone was quietly whispering his name behind his back, each one begging for the kind of special attention that only a vampire could give them. He felt slightly dizzy. He closed his eyes for a moment. When he opened them, the world seemed just a little bit steadier.

Leo and Annie had gone to get tickets – it seemed that, tonight, people *were* able to see Annie. It was often hard to tell: even when they couldn't actually *see* her, there was something about Annie's ghostly nature that made people avoid the empty bit of space where she stood. It was only in busy crowds, where people were jostling, that they ever stepped *through* her. And tonight didn't seem to be one of those nights.

'What a gentleman,' said Annie as she and Leo joined him and they headed in. 'Bought my ticket for me.'

Mitchell leaned in close.

'You do realise that you'll have to sleep with him now.'

'It's OK,' Annie said. 'I've told him you will.'

And with a cheeky grin she linked her arms with Mitchell's and Leo's.

Chapter
FIVE

Bite Me! were rubbish.

Well, that was what George thought. Although he wasn't quite sure whether his irritation with them was because of the music ('It's bloody loud!' he bellowed, only just audibly, into Mitchell's ear halfway through 'Body Of Evidence') or the caffeine. Or, more probably, to Kaz who was pogoing all over the place and quite clearly pissing off a few of the audience.

Gail tried to hold her down but she wasn't having any of it, braids flying everywhere, beads smacking everyone within a five-metre radius like miniature unguided missiles. If it weren't for the general feel-good atmosphere at the concert – the *gig* – Kaz would probably have been lynched.

'This is brilliant, yeah?' she whooped at George, waving her hands in the air, totally out of time to the music. George just nodded and realised he was clenching his jaw so hard that he was starting to get a headache. Why had no one told him about the side effects of frothy coffee?

George glanced over at Mitchell and Annie and Leo, a couple of metres away. At the bar, they'd made sure to keep Gail and Kaz well away from Leo – they couldn't work out how they could possibly introduce everyone without Leo wondering why Gail and Kaz weren't talking to Annie.

'We could pretend they've fallen out?' George had suggested as he passed squishy plastic glasses of beer to Mitchell. 'Say they've had some sort of spat?'

'And what happens if Leo gets chatting to them and decides to be a Good Samaritan and get them back together? "You two should come and talk to Annie." "Annie?" "Yeah, Annie – that friend of yours you've fallen out with – just over there." "Where?" "*There.*"' Mitchell pulled a face.

'See what you mean,' agreed George grudgingly. 'No way that's gonna end well, is there?'

So, as they squeezed their way through the crowd to get a better view near the front, George steered Gail and Kaz one way, and Mitchell took charge of Leo and Annie.

The support act – whose name George didn't even catch – had been even worse. Just lots of noise and shouting. *God!* thought George, slopping his beer down him as someone jostled him from behind. *I'm turning into my mother. Whatever happened to tunes and proper singing?*

He grunted as another shove from behind sent half his beer down the back of a small – but worryingly stocky – biker in front of him. George winced and was on the point of apologising to the bloke (who hadn't even noticed) when the man who'd bumped him tapped him on the shoulder.

'Sorry about that, mate,' he said as George turned.

'It's fine, really,' George started to apologise back. The man was a skinny, studenty-type with far too much black hair all swooshed round on his head and sunglasses on. *Indoors!*

'No, no, my fault. Let me get you another.' The man's eyes were invisible behind his sunglasses but he had a dazzlingly white smile that put George in mind of American film stars and people who spent far too much time thinking about their appearance.

'No, honestly, I'm fine,' insisted George, not wanting to make a scene.

'Lager, was it?'

The man seemed genuine enough and George nodded, realising that he wasn't going to take no for an answer.

'No probs – back in a sec.'

George turned back to watch the band on stage thrashing and leaping about, and cast a wary eye over the two groups of friends. Gail and Kaz seemed to be having a good time – especially Kaz. And Leo and Mitchell had their heads bent together and looked like they were comparing notes on the band.

'Here y'are,' said a voice behind George suddenly: it was the emo bloke, a new pint in his hand. That had been quick. George nodded and gave him a thumbs-up – and then had to knock back the remains of his first beer so that he wasn't standing there all night with both hands full. Too much caffeine and too much beer – great combination for a father-to-be. He caught Gail's eye and she gave him a big, warm smile. *Oh, sod it!* George thought, and chugged down the second pint.

An hour later, George was on top of the world. Something about the combination of beer and caffeine had sent a – well, the only word he could think of to describe it was a *whoosh!* – right through him. The music that, just half an hour earlier had been nothing but noise was suddenly a solid, gut-wrenching pulse inside of him. He'd never felt anything quite like it before – and boy was it *good*! He suddenly realised that he was bouncing away in time to the music. Actually *in time* to it. He caught Kaz looking at him.

'This is good!' he grinned, leaning over to her and shouting in her ear.

'You OK, yeah?' she asked, looking a bit concerned.

'I'm *brilliant!*' he laughed and downed the rest of his drink. 'What about you two?'

'Yeah, great,' Kaz said, but there was a bit of worry in her voice that he didn't quite get. 'Who's Mitchell's friend, then?'

'Ahhhh,' George said slowly. 'That's Leo.'

'And who's he?' Kaz winked.

'He's a mate of Mitchell's,' George said.

'Um, yeah, I get that bit.'

'He's not gay or anything,' George said hurriedly –
and then realised how loudly he'd said it and looked
around. But no one had heard him over the sound of
the band. 'Erm, d'you want another drink – I'm off to
the bar?'

Gail and Kaz wanted another couple of beers – and
so did Mitchell and Leo.

'You all right, George?' asked Mitchell as George
turned to go. 'You look a bit…'

'What? Like I'm having fun?'

Mitchell eyed him suspiciously.

'Well,' said George, overemphasising every word. 'I
am. Here y'are – finish this while I go to the bar.' He
thrust the remains of his last pint into Mitchell's hand
and set off for the bar.

For some reason, no one seemed quite as happy
as he felt – his smiles and nods at the audience were
greeted with slightly odd, reluctant ones. *Sod 'em!*
George thought as he finally popped out of the back
of the crowd and bounced towards the bar.

It was only as the drinks were lining up that he
realised that he didn't have enough hands to carry
them all, and he turned round, hoping to catch sight
of one of his friends to give him a hand.

'All right?' said a voice next to him.

It was the bloke with the sunglasses, flanked by two
other guys – a Chinese guy and another white one, all
of them, he now realised, dressed in black and wearing
sunglasses.

'You,' said George cheekily, 'look like the Men in
Black, you know.'

The first one grinned. 'Very flattering colour, black,' he said, flashing that whiter-than-white smile of his.

'Can I try your sunglasses on?' said George out of nowhere.

The three men exchanged glances, smiling at each other.

'Course you can, mate – here.'

He passed the sunglasses to George who put them on over the top of his own glasses, so that he could still see – and did a silly macho pose.

'Looking good,' said the Chinese guy, elbowing his mate. 'They suit him. Maybe he should join our gang. Whaddya reckon, Stu?'

Stu, the middle guy – the one who'd donated his sunglasses to George – pulled a thoughtful face.

'Maybe. A bit of a special club, though. Only the coolest dudes get to join.'

'Ah,' said George regretfully. 'Not very good at cool.'

'Oh, I dunno,' said the third guy appreciatively. 'You look pretty cool to me – whaddya think, guys? Is George cool enough to join our gang?'

'How d'you know my name?' asked George – more in amazement than anything.

'Heard your mates talking to you,' said Stu quickly.

George nodded. Seemed reasonable.

'And you're a pretty good dancer, too,' added Stu.

'I am not!' said George.

'Definitely.'

'Go on,' urged the third guy. 'Show us some moves.'

George went all bashful. 'Nah…'

'Go on,' said Stu. 'Gotta be able to dance to get in the cool club.'

There was something a bit weird about all of this, but George couldn't quite put his finger on what. The three blokes seemed friendly and up for a laugh – they'd even bought him a beer. And maybe George was cooler than he'd thought. He gave a little jiggle.

'See!' said Stu to his mates. 'Told you he could dance. Better not be *too* good, George. Don't want you stealing all our birds.'

'Yeah, right,' scoffed George, realising that he was still dancing.

The barman caught his attention and he started rooting round for his money, but Stu stepped in.

'On us,' he said with a wink.

'Nice one, thanks,' said George, shoving his money back in his pocket and dropping some loose change that went rolling away. 'Oops!'

The Chinese guy handed George one of the pints from the bar and he took it a bit unsteadily.

'Too much caffeine,' George said. 'Earlier.' He took a deep breath as he felt another wave of whooshiness come over him. 'Whoo!'

'You OK?' asked the third guy.

George nodded and handed the sunglasses back to Stu. He felt a little dizzy – not *bad* dizzy, sort of euphoric dizzy: bright and sharp. If this was what caffeine did to him, he could quite get used to it.

'Let's go over there,' suggested Stu, gesturing to one of the exits from the auditorium that led to the loos.

'Bit busy here.'

'OK,' agreed George, thinking that it wasn't actually that busy there at all.

The three of them went and stood in the doorway and waited for George to catch up. It suddenly dawned on George that he was doing that thing that everyone else did, and that had always come so hard to him: he was making friends! Cool friends. Even wearing sunglasses indoors didn't seem quite so twatty.

'You've stopped dancing,' Stu commented.

George pulled a face and took a gulp of his beer.

'Don't like this one so much.' He jerked his head in the direction of the band.

'Awwww,' the Chinese guy said, pulling a disappointed face. 'Go on – dance.'

'Yeah,' urged Stu. 'Dance for us.'

George rolled his eyes and suddenly realised that, somehow, they were out in the corridor. Cold fluorescents glared off white-painted breezeblock walls. He almost asked to borrow Stu's sunglasses again. The music seemed very distant – just an aching *thump thump thump* somewhere miles away.

'Dance, George!' said the third guy.

'Yeah, Georgie, dance!'

And suddenly all three guys were chanting 'Dance! Dance! Dance!' at him.

Part of him wanted to – part of him was still bouncing away in time to the distant music from the auditorium. But a part of him was just thinking 'This is *so* odd.' It was almost like he were looking at himself the wrong way down a telescope. He tried shuffling his feet as the three guys began to clap in time – claps that grew and grew in volume until they drowned out the sound of the music. Something was very strange. Very…

'George!'

George turned his head sharply: Mitchell was standing in the doorway, glowering at him.

'Mitchell!' George suddenly grinned, throwing his arms wide to hug his friend.

'What's going on, guys?' Mitchell asked, ignoring him now and staring at his new mates.

'Georgie here is giving us a little show,' said Stu.

'Yeah,' said the Chinese guy. 'A right little dancing doggie you've got here, Mitchell.'

Doggie? Mitchell?

What did they mean? How did they know –

With frightening speed, Mitchell threw himself at Stu and slammed him up against the wall, his forearm across the man's throat.

'Whoa!' said George – losing most of his beer to the floor as he forgot he was holding the plastic glass and it slopped everywhere. For some reason, the spilt beer seemed more important than what was going on with Mitchell and Stu. He stared at the puddle.

'Stay out of it, George,' Mitchell warned.

The third guy moved to pull Mitchell away, but something about Mitchell's expression made him think twice and he pulled back. The Chinese guy just looked awkward, glancing round.

'I don't know who you are,' Mitchell hissed. George could barely hear him. 'But I know *what* you are. And I know what you've done. George!' Mitchell barked.

'Go back inside.'

'Why?'

'Because, George…'

'Because what?'

'Because your mate Mitchell here doesn't like the idea of anyone having a good time apart from him,' said Stu, his voice choked by Mitchell's arm. 'He doesn't want you joining our gang. I think he wants to keep you for himself.' The Chinese guy laughed.

'Yeah – his own little pet.'

'Mitchell…' George protested, confused.

'They've spiked your drink, George,' Mitchell said.

'What?'

'They put E in your beer.'

George frowned. What was Mitchell on about? E? What?

'Just go back to the others, George,' Mitchell repeated, his voice level and sensible.

'But…' George gestured at the three blokes.

'George!'

'All right, all right,' said George, a bit miffed. He still didn't really know what was going on, but he wasn't so drunk – or whatever – that he couldn't pick up on the distinctly threatening vibes that he was picking up from the situation. But he couldn't leave Mitchell on his own, could he? Not if there was trouble.

'I'll get Leo,' he said brightly. Yes. Get Leo.

'No need,' came another voice – a rich, smooth, female voice. 'I think there are more than enough people at this party.'

George looked round. Standing about three metres

away in the middle of the corridor was a woman – a woman who looked completely out of place under the cold, sterile lights.

For a moment, George wondered if she were a tranny: she was very tall, black and incredibly striking. There was more than a hint of Grace Jones in her as she stood, weight on one hip, in a dark red, knee-length dress, buttoned diagonally across the breast.

She folded her arms and waited, like a school mistress who'd just shouted at a group of squabbling kids and was waiting for them to run off.

Mitchell pulled back from Stu who staggered to one side, rubbing his throat.

'Are these yours?' said Mitchell to the woman. 'You should learn to keep your dogs under control. Wouldn't want someone putting them down, would we?'

George was completely thrown. First Mitchell had a go at his mates and now this woman turned up. He felt like he'd missed an episode, somehow. He looked down at the puddle of split beer again.

'I'm still house-training them,' the woman said, arching an eyebrow. She jerked her head sharply and, muttering something George couldn't hear, George's three new friends slunk off down the corridor, casting murderous glances over their shoulders. George couldn't tell whether they were more pissed off with the woman or with Mitchell. He felt slightly sad to see them go.

'They spiked his drink,' Mitchell said, indicating George.

'I didn't mind,' protested George.

'Shut up, George.'

'I have shutted up.'

'So…?' Mitchell asked the woman.

'So?' The woman unfolded her arms and took a couple of precise steps towards the two of them. 'Just thought I'd say hello. I'm Olive – Olive King. A pleasure to meet you, Mitchell.'

She extended a hand with the reddest nails George had ever seen. For a second, he wanted to grab her hand and take a really, really, *really* close look. But that would just have been weird.

Mitchell ignored the outstretched hand. 'And that would be of interest to me – why, exactly?'

'Courtesy costs nothing, you know. You might say I'm the new girl in town. For a while, at any rate. The boys fancied a night out and, well, a band called Bite Me! is just too much of a temptation, isn't it – for people like us?'

The truth suddenly dawned on George and his mouth actually fell open.

'You're vampires, aren't you?' he exclaimed loudly – as Mitchell winced.

'George – please,' he said. 'Go back in there and find Kaz and Gail. They'll be wondering what's happened to us, and the last thing we want is them coming out here.'

George nodded thoughtfully. Made sense. Plus Bite Me! had moved onto another track, one that had got George's toes tapping again.

'You sure, Mitchell?' he said in a serious voice,

indicating Olive. 'Cos if you need me, you know, I'm always here for you.'

'George,' Mitchell said warmly, squeezing George's hand. 'Piss off.'

Annie was starting to get a bit worried – it had been over twenty minutes since George had vanished in search of beer, and ten since Mitchell had followed suit. She still couldn't work out what had happened: one minute Mitchell was finishing off the dregs of George's last drink and the next he'd sworn loudly, told her to keep Leo away from the dancing lesbians, and had stormed off, shoving his way through the crowd. Annie had horrible visions of finding him beaten up in a corner somewhere for spilling some drunken student's pint.

'What's happened to them two?' asked Leo.

Annie shrugged. 'Having a wee, I expect.'

'A long wee. George was getting the drinks in, wasn't he?' Leo said with a frown, downing the last of his beer and letting the plastic glass fall to the floor. Annie had to fight back the urge to pick it up and go find a bin for it. She caught sight of Kaz and Gail casting about, probably wondering where George had got to. She hoped they didn't decide to come and ask Leo, otherwise she suspected she'd have to make a swift exit.

'I'll go and find 'em,' Leo offered.

'I'll come with you,' Annie said, not wanting to be left in the crowd on her own. Leo led the way and Annie followed in his wake.

The two of them found themselves in the corridor leading to the loos. A couple of people were sitting on the floor, their backs to the walls, looking decidedly the worse for wear. But there was no sign of the two boys. Leo went into the men's loo to check, but came out shaking his head.

'Maybe Mitchell's gone out for a fag and taken George with him?'

'That's not like George – especially when it was his round. Oh,' she paused, a grin breaking out. 'Have I just answered my own question?'

'Nah,' Leo laughed. 'Georgie wouldn't wriggle out of his round – would he?'

No, thought Annie, he wouldn't. Not George's style. So where the hell were they?

George was confused. Three vampires had just spiked his drink (which, he supposed, might explain why he was feeling so good – but weren't spiked drinks supposed to be bad for you? Think about that one later, George), and then Mitchell had nearly had a fight with them, and then another vampire – a big, black lady vampire – had come along and scared them off. And now Mitchell was talking with the lady vampire. Yup, that seemed right. And yet, if it were, shouldn't he be feeling a bit more weirded out by it all? He just wanted to dance.

'Not a good time for thinking, George,' he said out loud to himself as he tried to remember where Kaz and Gail and Annie and Leo were. He wriggled his way through the crowd, finding an odd pleasure in the physical contact from squeezing past everyone (*It's the drugs, George. It's the drugs*) until he finally spotted Kaz and Gail.

Kaz seemed to have calmed down a bit, and they'd obviously been worried about him – which, thought George, was lovely, cos he'd been worried about them too – because the moment they saw him they grabbed him and demanded to know where he'd been and if he was all right and where Mitchell was.

'If I told you,' said George, raising his hands. 'I'd have to kill you. With hugs,' he added, throwing his arms around them both.

'Are you on drugs?' demanded Kaz, pulling back from him.

'Kaz,' said Gail patiently before George could say anything. 'This is George. Mitchell I could see taking drugs. But George…?'

George pulled a face and then realised that the last thing he wanted them to think was that he was full of E. Actually, no, he'd quite like to tell them – and see if he could get some for them, cos he just *knew* that they'd love it. But Kaz's scowling face stamped on that little dream pretty quickly – which suddenly filled him with a little wave of sadness. (*It's the drugs, George. It's the drugs.*)

'Beer!' he said suddenly and with absolute clarity. 'I was going to get beer! What happened to my beer?'

'George…?' Gail said in his ear. 'You're *not* on drugs, are you?'

He pulled back and stared her straight in the face. 'Yes!' he said.

Gail rolled her eyes, and then glanced at Kaz to see if she'd heard.

'I'm on the best drug there is,' he grinned. 'Love!'

As they were about to head back into the auditorium, having failed to find Mitchell and George, Leo suddenly clasped his hand to his stomach and let out a little moan.

'You OK?' Annie asked.

Leo nodded unconvincingly and managed a tight smile.

'What is it?' Annie put her hand on his arm but Leo just shook his head.

'Nah,' he said, waving her away. 'We're having a good night – don't want to spoil it.'

'Well if anything's guaranteed to spoil it, it's making a noise like that and pretending it's nothing.'

He gave a little laugh but a spasm of pain shot across his face again.

'Leo…' Annie said. 'What is it? Tell me.'

Leo took a breath and steadied himself against the wall as a couple of laughing girls came past, bottles of WKD in their hands, giggling. They gave him a sneery look – and, as soon as they got past, started giggling again.

'Has Mitchell not told you?'

'Told me what? Come on, sit down over here.'

She helped him over to a flight of steps and then snuggled in alongside him.

'Has Mitchell not told me what?' she repeated, looking him firmly in the eye.

'It's cancer,' he said with a wince.

'He did mention it, yeah. I'm so sorry.' Annie grabbed his hand and squeezed it. 'I didn't say anything in case it got Mitchell into trouble.'

'He's a cool bloke, isn't he?'

Annie pulled a face. 'Not sure cool's the word…' She smiled and squeezed Leo's hand again. 'But he's OK.'

'You known him for a while, then?'

'Oh, not all that long,' Annie said vaguely. It had become automatic with her to deflect conversations about the three of them. They always started off innocently enough, but their lives – separate and entangled – had enough potholes in them to trip a mountain goat up. She'd learned just to not go there.

'Mitchell's lucky to have friends like you, you know,' Leo said, watching a drunk-looking man stagger past. 'Shame I didn't meet you lot a while back – could have been fun. I can imagine me and Mitchell being best mates. You too. But…' He tailed off with a sigh.

'You're talking like you're already dead.'

Leo looked away.

'How bad is it, then? If you don't mind talking about it.'

Leo shrugged. 'They weren't sure until today – got the results of some tests back. Pancreatic. Looks like it's spread. Metasta-thingied.'

'Metastasized?'

He nodded. 'The little buggers are all over the place now.'

'Oh, Leo,' said Annie, putting her arm around his shoulder. 'I'm sorry.'

'All gotta go sometime, haven't we?'

Have we? she thought.

'What have...' She floundered around for the right words. 'How long have they said? Sorry, sorry – I'm getting all nosey now, aren't I?'

'No, no – it's all right. Can't keep it all bottled up inside me, can I?' He fixed her with his pale blue eyes. 'That's not what friends do.'

She squeezed his hand again.

'Six months, maybe. A year tops.'

'God.'

Leo nodded. 'But life goes on...' He laughed, hollowly. 'Or it doesn't.'

'Who knows, though?' Annie said, trying to be upbeat. 'Sometimes these things sort themselves out, go into remission, don't they? And no one knows why. Mind over matter, I suppose.'

'Gonna need an awful lot of that.'

'Well, we're here for you.'

'Thanks, Annie.'

Leo suddenly leaned forward and threw his arms around her, and they sat in a silent hug for a while.

'Right,' said Leo, pulling away with a deep breath. 'Enough of my miseries. Let's go and find the others. They'll think we're shagging in the toilets.'

'I'm sorry about George, by the way,' said Olive as George vanished. 'They're new converts, the boys. Youthful high spirits.'

'Like I say,' Mitchell said, his voice low. 'Keep them under control or *I* will.'

Olive paused for a moment, looking him up and down. 'Understood.'

Mitchell nodded.

'Here,' she said, offering him a business card. 'My number.'

Mitchell frowned. 'And I'd want it why, exactly?'

Olive gave a tiny shrug. 'Who knows what life might throw at us? Let's just say you might need a friend at some point.'

'I have all the friends I need, thanks.'

She considered what he'd said. 'Maybe. But friendship's sometimes the flipside of enmity, isn't it? Like love and hate. Sometimes hard to separate out the two.' She flashed a brilliant smile at him. 'Anyway, enjoy the rest of your evening.'

Olive turned and walked away, heels clicking on the corridor floor.

As she vanished from sight, Mitchell let out a sigh and sagged against the wall. He could still feel the adrenalin, pumping away inside of him, his heart racing. What the hell had that all been about? Had Olive and her poodles been there for a night out, or had they been there to look out for him and George? Mitchell shook his head – paranoia, here we come.

Chapter
Six

Annie and Leo were sitting on the steps outside. Leo had bummed a cigarette off one of the students, and Annie was trying – and failing – to convince him that, in his condition, smoking wasn't the best idea he'd had all night.

'Reckon it's a bit late for worrying about fags,' he told her.

Annie wasn't sure what to say to that. Once his 'poorly fit' – as he'd called it – was over and he'd drunk some water, he'd seemed much better, and Annie had suggested they come and get some fresh air: the gig had been winding up as they'd gone back into the auditorium and already people were starting to leave, so they just went with the flow.

'So what's the Leo story, then?' Annie asked.

'The Leo Story? Huh – I reckon it's one of those

rubbishy British comedies that no one actually laughs at.'

'Is that how you cope with it?' Annie shook her head. 'Sorry – you barely know me and already I'm giving you the third degree.'

'First degree, second degree, third degree... doesn't bother me,' he laughed. 'Got married, no kids, wife met someone else, split up. End of, really. Lost my job.' He shrugged. 'Shit happens.' He grinned ruefully and flicked his ciggie out into the dark.

'God, I know how to kill a party, don't I?' Annie sighed. 'Owen always said...'

She stopped and stared into the night.

'Who's Owen? Ex?'

'Yeah. We were – Mitchell!'

Annie was almost relieved when Mitchell suddenly appeared out of nowhere. He looked edgy and agitated, looking round with a deep frown on his face.

'You two OK?'

'Fine, mate, fine,' said Leo with a wink. 'Just chatting about stuff. Good night, yeah?'

Mitchell nodded noncommittally, still checking out the crowds streaming out into the damp night.

'Where's George?' Annie glanced back up the steps, but there was no sign of George or the others.

'Must be on the way out,' Mitchell said. 'No sign of him in there.'

'What's up?' asked Annie solicitously. 'You look a bit...'

Mitchell gave her his warmest, fakest smile. 'It's nothing – just want to know that everyone's OK.' He peered at Leo, silhouetted against the light. 'Leo?'

Annie glanced at him – he looked a bit healthier than he had done ten minutes ago, but he was still pretty pale.

'It's nothing,' Leo said. 'Just felt a bit gippy back there. Annie got me some water – I'm fine now.'

'Sure?'

Leo nodded. He glanced at his watch. 'S'pose I'd better be off.'

Annie reacted before her common sense could kick in. 'Come back to ours!'

Leo glanced up at Mitchell. 'Oh, I dunno…'

'Oh, go on,' said Annie. 'It'd be nice – chilling out and all that. Just for a bit. Mitchell?' After Leo's confession earlier, she didn't think they could just abandon him to go back to his flat on his own. If it had been her that had just received the news Leo had done, the last thing she'd want would be to be alone.

'Well…' said Mitchell awkwardly.

'No, it's OK, mate,' said Leo, getting stiffly to his feet. 'It's fine. Wouldn't want to spoil a great night.'

'Oh shut up,' Annie said. 'Come on. You can get a cab from ours later.'

'You sure?' Leo looked at Mitchell for confirmation.

He eventually nodded. 'But listen – don't make too much of this, but someone spiked George's drink in there.'

'They *what*?' said Annie, aghast.

'It's OK, he's fine – just a bit loved-up. Don't go on about it, cos it'll just make him feel weirder about it – but I thought you should know.'

'So I don't think he's coming on to me when he gets all huggy?' Leo grinned. 'Nice one. Cheers. Thanks for the invite, and mum's the word about the drugs. To be honest, the thought of going back to my flat right now...' He scowled. 'Not really grabbing me. Thanks.'

Leo put his arm around Mitchell and Annie's shoulders and gave them a squeeze. Annie, however, was too preoccupied with Mitchell's revelation about George's drink getting spiked. She wanted to ask Mitchell if he knew who'd done it, but there was something about the way Mitchell was treating it that suggested he didn't want a big discussion about it. Not here, at any rate.

They heard George before they saw him: his cry of 'Mitchell! Annie!' would have been enough to wake the dead and, for a moment, Annie wondered whether she'd actually be able to cope with him once they got him home. He gave them both – and Leo – another hug. She hadn't known quite what to expect: George on the floor in a puddle of his own sick? Thrashing about, having some sort of fit, in a toilet cubicle? She certainly hadn't expected the grinning bundle of joy that stood in front of her.

'Where are the lovebirds?' asked Mitchell, scanning the departing crowds for Kaz and Gail.

'Oh, they've pulled,' said George blithely. 'Mitchell, those—'

'They've *what*?' cut in Annie.

'Oh, not *pulled* pulled. They've got chatting to some

students and they're off to the bar – I said we'd meet them there.' His face suddenly brightened as a thought occurred to him: 'Can we go clubbing?'

'On a Tuesday night?' Mitchell said dubiously.

'I thought Bristol was the city that never slept,' George countered.

'That's Bath,' Leo laughed.

'Well,' said Annie, standing up. 'We thought we'd all go back for a nightcap. Leo's coming.'

George looked torn – he obviously didn't want the night to end just yet. He glanced at Mitchell, and a fleeting frown crossed his face. He opened his mouth to say something and promptly shut it again.

'Right – casting vote,' said Mitchell decisively 'You're coming back. If we leave you with those two, you'll end up getting drunk and you'll be a dad sooner than you expected. And if you promise to keep the noise down, we'll let you put something shite and dancey on when we get back.'

George looked at him and grinned. 'Yay!' He swung his hips from side to side, and Annie covered her face in embarrassment.

'I'm gonna be a dad,' he said stupidly.

'Yes,' said Mitchell. 'You're gonna be a dad. And we're all very happy for you. Now let's get a taxi before we freeze to death!'

George was still pretty loved-up as they staggered in. Mitchell headed straight for the fridge and got them some beers while Annie put the kettle on. George headed straight to the hi-fi and managed to find something vaguely dancey. As it blared out at full volume, Mitchell had to race over to turn it down. They'd had enough run-ins with the neighbours. They didn't need another one. George pulled a sulky face and rolled his eyes. He hadn't said anything about Olive and her boys – which, in front of Leo, could have been a disaster. Truth be told, he was actually quite liking druggy George: there was a warmth and openness that was quite appealing.

When Mitchell had finished George's beer off, back at the gig, he'd instantly known that something was wrong with it: one of the perks of being a vampire – enhanced taste and smell. He'd caught the sharp whiff of MDMA along with a tiny bit of ketamine and some speed. Not a lethal mix by any drug-taker's standards; not even a particularly powerful mix. But for someone like George who wasn't used to the stuff…

'Here y'are, mate,' Leo said, handing him a beer and looking round the lounge appreciatively.

'Nice place – just the three of you, then?'

Mitchell nodded, keeping an eye on George who was standing in the middle of the floor, his eyes shut, slopping his beer all over the carpet as he danced out of time to 'Rhythm Is A Dancer'.

'So what's the story?'

'Us three? Oh,' he said drily. 'Just three lost souls drawn together by our mutual love and desperation.'

'No one else would have us,' added Annie, bringing in a tray with four mugs of tea and a sugar bowl. 'Life's rejects, us.'

'Looks like I'm in good company, then – cheers!'

Leo raised his bottle and clinked it with Mitchell and George. Annie, not wanting to be left out, grabbed a mug of tea and joined in. She was glad they'd invited Leo back: the thought of him sitting in his flat, all alone, thinking about his diagnosis didn't bear thinking about.

'So what was all that about being a dad?' Leo asked, sinking back into the sofa as Annie fished around in a cupboard for some candles, just to give the place a bit more atmosphere. George was still jigging about in the middle of the room.

'Sit down, George,' Annie said. 'You look like some sort of weird, spaced-out go-go dancer.'

George just grinned and stuck two fingers up at her.

'Ignore her,' he said to Leo, his eyes wide. 'She's just jealous cos *I'm gonna be a dad* and she's not.'

'George,' Annie warned him. 'Sit down or the three of us will shove your bits in the blender, and then you'll never be a dad.'

George settled for plonking himself on the arm of the sofa, dancing from the waist up and doing something ridiculous with his arms.

'George,' said Mitchell, 'is going to be a dad. Did he mention that?'

'Congratulations, mate,' Leo said, reaching out and clinking beer bottles. 'Nice one. Who's the lucky girl?' He threw a glance at Annie who pulled a *never in a million years* face.

'The lovely lesbian Gail,' George said. 'Lovely, luscious, lesbian Gail. The lovely, luscious, lesb—'

'Shut up,' said Annie.

George slapped his hand over his own mouth.

Leo looked puzzled.

Mitchell stepped in to explain. 'Gail and Kaz have been wanting a kid for a while, and last week, George here accidentally promised that he'd be happy to donate some jizz for them.'

'And they say romance is dead,' Annie said.

'Sperm-hungry lesbians, eh?' laughed Leo. 'Think I've got the DVD back at my flat.'

Annie slapped his leg.

'Sorry,' Leo apologised. 'So when's it due?'

'Oh, they've not "done the deed" yet,' Mitchell said. 'It was only yesterday that Kaz sprang it on him.'

'She did not,' George said indignantly, almost falling off the arm of the sofa.

'She did, George – remember.'

George thought for a minute. 'Oh yeah.'

'So it's a turkey-baster job, is it?' Leo said with a smile. 'You go round there, pop to the loo and do the business and then hand it over to the ladies?'

George considered Leo's précis. 'Yup,' he said. 'That's about the size of it.'

'Bad choice of words, George,' laughed Mitchell. 'Although on second thoughts…'

'Oi!' said George. 'I'll have you know I'm pretty well—'

'La la la la!' said Annie loudly, clapping her hands over her ears. 'Too much information! Too much information!'

The rest of them collapsed in giggles.

Leo fetched them some more beers from the fridge.

'Not drinking your tea?' he asked Annie when he came back.

'She has this thing,' Mitchell said. 'Sort of OCD. You've no idea how many teabags we get through around here.'

The conversation turned to a discussion of the house's music collection – with George defending all the rubbish (most of it his) and Mitchell and Leo comparing stories about the '80s. It turned out that Leo had something of an encyclopaedic knowledge of music from that era, and he and Mitchell set about trying to prove who knew most.

Annie kept sneaking glances at Leo, just to check he was OK. After the incident at the gig, she was a bit worried about him. She had no idea exactly how far the cancer had spread, and it didn't seem like the kind of thing she could drill him about. But he seemed fine, if a little tired.

About 2 a.m., he started yawning and looked at his watch.

'Hell,' he said. 'Sorry – lost track of the time.' He heaved himself – a little unsteadily – out of the sofa and stood wobbling, looking round for his jacket. 'Better call a cab.'

'You might as well stay here,' Annie found herself saying. Mitchell threw her a look – which dissolved into a nod.

'Don't want to put you out,' he said.

'Have my bed,' George volunteered, tipping the last of his beer down his throat and opening another one.

'I'm not going to be going to bed for…' He puffed out his cheeks. 'For ever, probably.'

Leo shook his head.

'You've already been—'

But George lunged across and clamped a hand over Leo's mouth. 'George has spoken,' he said, a little slurrily. 'Bed. Now.'

'George can be very masterful when he wants,' Mitchell said. 'It's just that he doesn't often want to be.'

'Well, if you're sure,' Leo said.

George nodded intently. 'I'm sure. Come on – I'll show you where it is.'

'And hide your mucky pants,' Annie added. 'That room's a tip.'

George rolled his eyes as he followed Leo upstairs. 'Yes, Mum.'

'So…' said Mitchell with more than a twinkle in his eye as George and Leo headed upstairs.

'So what?'

He gave Annie one of those sly, sidelong looks.

'What?'

'Leo.'

'What about—' Annie's mouth dropped open. 'Oh, you are kidding, aren't you?'

'Stranger things have happened.'

'Like?'

'Like a dead woman, a vampire and a werewolf sharing a house in Bristol.'

'Trust me,' Annie said, gathering up the mugs.

'There's strange and there's *strange*. And the thought of me and Leo is most definitely *strange*. He's a nice bloke, but I reckon you two stand more chance of getting it on than me and him.'

'What?' Mitchell was agog.

'In the taxi on the way back, you were, like "Oh, Mitchell, d'you remember *this* film? Wasn't it cool!" And "Oh Leo, I love this band, don't you?",' Annie mocked as she headed into the kitchen.

'He's a nice guy that's having a hard time at the moment, is all,' Mitchell said defensively. He could hear the sound of the kettle starting up.

Annie came back in and plonked herself down on the sofa. 'He got his results today,' she said quietly.

'Who?'

'Leo.'

'What results?'

Annie gave him a hard stare. 'His cancer,' she said pointedly. 'It's not good news.'

'Shit. I'd almost forgotten. Is that where you two were when you vanished?'

Annie nodded and pulled her knees up, hugging them to her. 'We think we've got it bad.'

'You'd prefer cancer?'

'Dunno.' She went silent for a moment. In the background, the Thompson Twins wondered about whether it was love they were feeling. 'No,' she said eventually. 'I suppose not. We all want what we don't have, don't we? Or don't want what we do have.'

'Well,' said Mitchell after a suitable pause. 'Way to bring the party down.'

'Is that all you think about?' Annie was suddenly angry. 'Party party party?'

'Course it's not. Just that I thought we were having a good night – celebrating George's impending mistake.'

Annie turned to him sharply. 'You just can't do it, can you?'

'Do what?'

'Be happy. Let other people be happy. You just can't.'

'Jesus,' hissed Mitchell, rubbing his eyes. 'All I said was—'

'If it's not what Mitchell wants then it's a bad thing.'

'Where the hell's all this coming from?'

Annie shook her head. 'It's not coming from anywhere. It's just... why are you always so *cynical* about everything? Why can't you just accept that, yes, our lives – if you can call them that – are never going to be normal. They're never going to be perfect. So why not just grab a bit of happiness when we can? And let other people have theirs.'

'Is this about George?'

'It's about all of us, Mitchell. It's about you, doing your father thing.'

'My *what*?' Mitchell was gobsmacked: what the hell had happened to his evening in the last few seconds?

'Your father thing,' Annie was saying. 'Always on the lookout for us doing the wrong thing, always ready to wade in and point out that we shouldn't be doing it.'

'Well maybe this house needs someone who's going to do that.'

'Since when?'

Mitchell gritted his teeth. 'Since we all started living together. It might have escaped your attention, but this isn't exactly *Man About The House.*'

'Man about the what?'

'Annie, you like to think this is a normal house with three normal people living in it, but it's not. And if you think we can all get along if we just put on a smile, we can't. There are people out there, Annie, who would kill me and George if they knew what we were. They would *kill us*. Jesus, haven't you learned anything? You're already dead – it's not like anything worse can—'

Mitchell stopped. Annie was staring at him, her lips drawn into a tight line. For a moment, he didn't know if she was going to cry or scream or hit him.

'Thanks,' she said in a thin, brittle voice. 'Thanks for reminding me of that, Mitchell. Cos it's really easy for me to forget, isn't it? What with me having such a normal life.'

'I didn't mean—'

'Hello?' It was George, peering around the bottom of the stairs with a very worried look on his face. 'Turn my back for two minutes… What's up?'

Mitchell and Annie looked at each other. Mitchell was on the point of making light of it all, telling George that they were just messing about. But he realised that his and Annie's spat was just a symptom of stuff that had been going on for weeks. And George's announcement of his decision to become a dad was the final cherry on the cake. Maybe things needed saying.

'Annie here thinks that I piss on everyone's parades. Isn't that right, Annie?'

George threw himself into the armchair. 'I knew it was too good to last,' he said, taking his glasses off. He breathed on them slowly and carefully, before polishing them on his shirt. 'Come on, then.' He put them back on and fixed them both with a steely – if slightly wild – glare. 'Let's get it out of the way. I'm full of love and drugs so you'll probably have an easy ride. This is about me and the baby, isn't it?'

'This is about all of us and the baby,' Mitchell said. He paused, expecting an outraged outburst from George. But George just nodded. *Thank God for 3,4-methylenedioxymethamphetamine.*

'Go on,' George said. 'Take advantage of me while you can. I'm listening.'

Mitchell took a deep breath.

'Us,' he said. 'The three of us. We're not like normal people, normal housemates. We aren't just living here together cos we're at the same uni, or cos we work together. We're living together because there's nowhere else for us. This is it.' He gestured around the room. 'This is our safe space, our own little world where we can be honest about who and what we are. Out there, we can work and we can play and we can pretend. But it's only in here that we can be *us*. And I'm not going to see that threatened.' He shook his head, watching George carefully. 'Of course I want you to be happy, George. God, there's nothing more I want than for us *all* to be happy. But we need to look at the bigger picture.' He turned to Annie. 'If that makes me some sort of bossy, domineering dad, then maybe that's because we need someone to do that.'

'Why?' asked George simply.

'Because we're not normal. We're freaks. Freaky stuff happens around us. Have you forgotten all the shit that's happened to us since we moved in together? And in case you need reminding, George, three vampires spiked your drink this evening and if it hadn't been for—'

'Three what?' cut in Annie, looking at Mitchell and then at George and then at Mitchell again. '*Vampires*?'

Mitchell sagged in his seat. 'I wasn't going to say anything,' he sighed.

Annie glared at George. 'Is that true?'

George nodded.

'Bloody hell,' Annie said. 'Why?'

'They were playing with him,' Mitchell said. 'With *us*. If I hadn't tasted it in George's beer, God knows what would have happened.'

'They might have given me some more,' said George, mock-glumly.

'George, this isn't funny.' Annie shook her head.

'Well maybe that's an argument for us not living together,' George said reasonably. 'Maybe if freaky stuff keeps happening to us we need to ask ourselves why. Maybe it's *because* we're living together.'

'You're serious?' This was so not the direction Mitchell had expected the conversation to take.

George held his gaze for a moment. 'No,' he said

softly, closing his eyes and tipping his head back. 'Not really.'

'Hang on,' said Annie thoughtfully. 'Maybe George is right. Maybe we're all just living here, sticking with each other, because we're too scared to think about what would happen if we didn't. And maybe that's unhealthy. Maybe we've all just got used to living like this because it's easier than *not* living together.' She pulled a thoughtful face and nodded. 'Maybe George is right,' she said again.

'I'm not,' George insisted gently. 'I've just said. But if you think this baby is going to come between us, then maybe it's time *I* looked for somewhere else to live.'

Mitchell shook his head and clenched his fists. 'Don't be such an arse, George. That's not what I'm saying. I'm just... I'm just looking out for us. That's all. We all look out for each other in different ways, and this is just the way I do it. And believe me, this baby's going to be a big thing – for all of us. So if I feel like it might threaten what we have here—'

'Threaten?' George's voice was calm and controlled but he was ramping up the volume. '*Threaten*? What are you talking about, Mitchell? This is a baby that's not even been conceived, never mind *born*. How the hell is it going to *threaten* us?'

Mitchell leaned forwards on the sofa. He kept his voice low, aware that Leo was upstairs asleep. The last thing he wanted was for a complete stranger to wake up in the middle of all of this.

'What if – just for example – it turns out that your

condition *is* genetic? Some weird stuff that doesn't show up on tests, yeah? What if everything seems normal and then the baby's born.' He paused. 'And it's not. Think about it, George. Before you know it, the hospital's on to Kaz and Gail, and they tell them that you're the father and then they start investigating *you*, trying to find out why little whatever-it's-called is getting a bit more than colic every full moon. And they start digging a bit more – looking into the bloke you share a house with, the one that doesn't like being photographed or videoed. The one that doesn't actually have a reflection. And while they're poking around, some of them notice Annie – a woman who's technically dead. What happens then, George?'

George reached for one of the unopened bottles of beer on the table – and changed his mind.

'That's a pretty good case,' he said thoughtfully. 'For not living together. Or at least for me not living here. Don't you think?'

'It's *not*,' said Mitchell through gritted teeth. 'It's a case for us being careful – for us looking out for each other, like tonight. For us being honest with each other.'

'And being honest and careful, in this case, means telling Kaz that it's all off and that Gail has to go find someone else.' George's voice was calm and measured. 'And me accepting that that's it – that I'm never going to have kids cos maybe, just maybe, they might turn out like me.'

Mitchell didn't know what to say. It was an awful, horribly perfect summation.

But George hadn't finished.

'I take it you feel the same about anyone else with some sort of genetic condition, do you? That they shouldn't be allowed to breed in case they have "defective" kids.' George indicated the quote marks in the air with his fingers.

Mitchell looked at Annie, but she was staring at George.

'And what about *you*, Mitchell?' George's voice was flat and calm.

'What about me?'

'You've always used condoms, have you? Always practised safe sex?'

'That's different.'

'Is it?' George raised his eyebrows. 'How much do you know about vampirism?' He pronounced the word carefully, using it like a knife, slowly dissecting Mitchell's argument. 'How certain are you that it can't be spread sexually? One hundred per cent? Ninety-nine per cent? What's an acceptable percentage, Mitchell? Or maybe it's not about percentages. Maybe it's just about what Mitchell wants. Cos that's what it seems to come down to.'

'What are you on about, George?'

'Are you really worried about what might happen to us? Or is it about what might happen to you?'

Mitchell didn't understand.

'Maybe you're just scared that if our happy little home all fell apart that you'd be out there on your own. Back to your old ways.'

'Too right I'm scared of that. Wouldn't you be?'

'You think I don't know that, Mitchell? You think me
and Annie aren't scared when we think about what's
going to happen to us?' George rubbed his forehead.
'You two – all this.' He looked around the room. 'Apart
from Nina, this is the best thing that's happened to me
since... since Tully infected me. But it's not for ever, is
it?'

'What d'you mean?'

'It's not for ever. It's now. It's for a few weeks or a
few months or a few years. But it's not for ever. Sooner
or later something's going to happen.' He looked at
Annie. 'One day, that door's going to open for Annie
and she'll be gone. One day you're going to get bored,
Mitchell – no, don't say anything. One day you're
going to get bored with living with me in this place.
You've travelled the world, Mitchell. You've already
lived longer than me and Annie combined. You'll be
off. Whether it's a woman or a job or whatever. One
day you'll be off. This... this is just the blink of an eye
to you.'

Annie shook her head. 'But...' was all that she could
manage.

'He's right,' Mitchell said gently, cutting in. 'George
is right. Six months, a year. Ten years. For me it's just
the blink of an eye.' He raised his palms. 'I can't argue
with that.'

'And sooner or later you'll get bored,' George said.
'You'll move on. And what's left for me when you're
gone? I met Nina – and look what happened there.'

'There'll be others,' Annie said quickly.

'No,' said George. 'That's the point. There won't be.

There *can't* be. I can't do that to someone again.'

'But you don't know–'

'I *do*.' George jabbed at the arm of the sofa with controlled precision. 'I know that as long as I've got this… this *thing* in me I can't be *normal*. None of us can be *normal*, but we've all got to handle it differently.' He looked up at the two of them. 'What's the lifespan of a werewolf?'

The sudden question threw Mitchell. Annie saw him shrug.

'Exactly,' said George. 'Wolves live about ten or fifteen years – maybe up to twenty in captivity. I looked it up. So what does that say about me, about how long I'll live for? Split the difference – die at, what, fifty? Or maybe I'll live a normal, human lifespan. Eighty or ninety years, say. Maybe I'm immortal like Mitchell. When will I find that out? Yes, I think I'm getting older but I don't *know*, do I? I can't live for a load of maybes and perhaps.'

George's hands went to his face, covering his eyes.

'And more than anything,' he said, a tremor in his voice, 'I don't want to be 50 and alone and unloved with no one around me because I haven't dared let anyone get close.' George began to cry softly. 'And I *can't* let anyone get close, because if I do they'll end up like Nina. Or they'll find out and they'll leave me. Or they'll find out and they *won't* leave me and I'll think they're staying out of pity. I can't do that. What's the point of it all if that's how it's going to be?' He took the handkerchief that Annie was offering him and snuffled into it. 'Just getting up and eating and working and checking my pubes every day to see if there are any grey ones and if I'm actually *getting* older. And once a month I lock myself away from normal people so that I don't kill anyone.' He looked up at them. 'When do I start *living*, eh?'

Mitchell didn't know what to say.

'This baby,' continued George. 'This baby is a chance for me to have something normal – something that's mine. Something to love, and to love me, to look after me when I'm old and shitting myself and asking everyone why you don't see Bruce Forsyth on the telly any more. Can't you see that? This arrangement, this thing with Gail and Kaz – it's perfect.' He gave a snotty laugh. 'OK, perfect might be pushing it. But think about it: whoever he or she is, they won't be living here, not with me. They won't be in any danger. They'll have two parents who love them, and Gail and Kaz have said I can get involved as much as I want in bringing them up.' George was smiling now, even though his eyes were still glistening. He sniffed back a few more tears. 'Can't I have just a taste of normality. Can't I put something back into the world that isn't just killing and death. And it's not just about a life for a life and all that bollocks. It's not about making up for killing Herrick. It's not even about making up for Nina. It's about...' George looked at Mitchell. 'You might not understand this, Mitchell. But it's about having my *own* little bit of immortality. It's about knowing that I had a purpose in life, something beyond me. Something that'll be there when I've gone that isn't an autopsy report about a man found shredded in a wood somewhere.'

'Immortality's not all it's cracked up to be,' Mitchell said sourly. 'Believe me.'

'Maybe not *your* kind of immortality, and maybe not for *you*. But for the rest of us…'

Annie stretched out a hand and took George's.

'Maybe you're right. Maybe we're programmed like that, programmed to do what we can to make sure we have our own little piece of immortality.'

A thoughtful silence fell. Mitchell didn't know what to say: here they were, three people brought together by the way life had messed them all up, and no matter how close they came to seeing the world through each other's eyes, none of them could really understand how the others felt.

'That's why,' George said brightly, breaking the quiet 'I've got an appointment tomorrow – to see a doctor.'

'What?' said Mitchell. 'What kind of a doctor?'

'A medical doctor.'

Mitchell glared at him. 'At the hospital?'

George shook his head. 'It's a private clinic – a Doctor Hardimann, I think. Down on Pembroke Road. Gail and Kaz are paying.' He looked up at them both and gave a lopsided grin. 'Kaz started to complain about the cost but Gail shut her up. Don't ever, ever tell them, but I'm glad it's Gail that's having the baby and not Kaz.'

'But there's no guarantee that they'll pick it up, whatever it is,' said Mitchell, still unconvinced, still the voice of reason.

'If there *is* anything to pick up,' Annie pointed out.

'Nope, you're right.' George gave one last blow into

the hanky. 'There's no guarantee. No guarantee at all.'

He raised his eyebrows and purposefully opened another beer, raising it in the air.

'Welcome to life, Mitchell.'

VAUXHALL, LONDON

Right, let me get this straight – if you'll pardon the pun. I'm not gay. I'm not even bi. They say that everyone's on a spectrum from 100 per cent gay at one end to 100 per cent straight at the other, but that almost no one is exclusively one or the other.

Well sorry, but I'm obviously one of the almost-no-ones. It doesn't repulse me. I don't get all hetero and thuggish about gays, none of that silly attitude. When you've lived as long as I have, you see stuff like that for the tiny-minded crap that it is. Eternity gives you a whole new perspective on things. Everyone should try it…

But really – never been with a bloke, never want to. I'm not saying that it'll never happen – hell, 80 years ago if you'd asked me whether I'd have chosen to become a vampire I'd have laughed you out of the room. Never say never. But it's not going to happen any time soon.

So, you may ask yourselves, what am I doing in a notorious gay fetish club in London?

Simple – I'm having a night out with some mates.

Yes, even vampires have friends.

Surprised? I bet you thought we were just cold, solitary creatures of the night, living in grotty garrets, slinking through the dark streets to return before dawn, spattered with the blood of our victims.

Welcome to the twentieth century.

Of course we have friends. We're, ahem, human, after all. We like a chat and a pint and a night in watching the telly. We have jobs, we go on holiday. OK, so we have slightly different feeding habits to the rest of humanity, and we're theoretically immortal. But there's an awful lot of time to fill between kills. We need something to do.

And like I said before, I've got no problem with gays – or, as I've been told I should call them, 'gay men'. It's all PC bollocks I think – but hey, if that's what they want to be called, who am I to argue? So Joe and Paul fancied a night out at this place and asked me if I wanted to come along. I was a bit iffy at first but, hey, you gotta give it a go. Joe and Paul have been a couple for about sixty years – and neither of them looks a day over 25. (Maybe they're not actually vampires but just use a lot of moisturiser?) They've been coming to this place for a couple of years now, and thought I'd enjoy it.

And, y'know, they weren't wrong.

The crowd were virtually all men, of course – a couple of women but they're clearly into other women and a bit too tattooed for my tastes. But the music's good and there's a really heavy vibe in the air that's certainly doing it for me.

The club is huge, lots of dark corners and winding corridors; couples snogging – and more – everywhere you look. And even though I say it myself, I'm getting quite a few looks. Must be the hair – in fact I probably have more hair on my head than anyone else here, and that includes the women. Makes me a bit different. And I think the aloofness helps: I'm not giving out the waves of desperation that some of them are. I feel special. Different. I am special and different. I'm liking this.

Paul and Joe have taken some muscled guy into a corner. Brawn, not brains. Wise choice. The last time I passed, they were chowing down on either side of his neck. He had his head tipped back, eyes shut. He looked to be enjoying it. A 'pain pig', Joe called him later. Always a good choice. You can get away with murder with a guy like that. Almost.

I caught the two of them coming out of the toilets, having cleaned the blood from their lips, hand in hand. They gave me the thumbs-up.

I saw the guy later, being helped into an ambulance, a torn T-shirt wrapped around his neck like some weird, tie-dyed scarf. They hadn't gone 'all the way' with him, hadn't killed him. We don't always, you know. People think that that's all we're after – blood and death. That'd just be mad – think of the attention we'd attract. Sometimes you just want a light snack, something to take the edge off the hunger. Of course I can't deny that a full kill is so much more satisfying – taking them right to the edge, holding them there, just for a few seconds, and then…

But variety is the spice of life, isn't it?

Seeing the two of them with the muscle guy made me feel a bit peckish, I can tell you. And although there's not a gay bone in my body (yes, yes) I started looking around for someone. And I found him: a thin guy, shaved head – barely a meal in him, if you ask me. But there was something hard in his eyes, something about the assortment of metalwork that pierced his eyebrow and lip and nipples that brought the guys' 'pain pig' phrase to mind.

Go on, *I thought.* Give it a go.

Don't get me wrong – I'd fed on men before. Sometimes you don't have much choice: when the hunger calls, it calls. But it's always a quick kill. In and out. None of the flirting, the eye contact, the sensuality that comes with a woman. Not my bag, as they say.

I stopped and leaned against the wall in the entrance to one of the dark cubbyholes that lined the place. From inside I could hear grunting, smell sweat. Sex. The guy drifted past, hard eyes on mine, no trace of a smile. I could see the hunger on his face – a different hunger to mine, but not so different. And I reckon he saw mine. He stopped, right in front of me, face just inches away. For a few seconds, he just stared into my eyes, before moving in for a kiss.

I turned my head away – gently, of course. Didn't want to scare him off, did I? He took that as a sign to begin kissing my neck. And just for a moment, I nearly walked away from it all, I really did. It just felt wrong. Not bad, just wrong. For me. He obviously felt me tense up and gently pushed me into the darkness of the cubbyhole.

Oh well, *I thought.* In for a penny...

So I tipped my head and I bit into his neck.

I thought he was going to scream, push me away, run off – hit me even. Instead, after the initial tensing, I felt him relax, heard a thin sigh escape his lips. I don't think he knew quite how deeply I'd bitten — they often don't, you know. Something about getting caught up in the moment. You'd be surprised how easy it is to break the skin, to puncture veins and arteries without the victim thinking you're doing anything more than giving them a love bite.

I felt myself shudder as the blood trickled into my mouth and he pulled me onto him, his hand around the back of my head, fingers locked in my hair, forcing me onto him, into him.

Jesus.

Chapter
SEVEN

George woke up on the sofa and lay there for a few moments, staring up at the grubby ceiling, wondering whether the drugs had worn off yet. A tiny, tiny part of him hoped that they hadn't – that he'd leap off the sofa, full of energy and bounce. But the fact that he just wanted to lie there, warm and quiet, told him that they had. Ho hum.

Despite all the stuff with the vampires and the conversation with Annie and Mitchell about the baby, he couldn't help but think it had actually been a good night. In fact he couldn't remember the last time he'd had quite such a good one.

He stretched out a bit and pulled the blanket that Mitchell had fetched for him up to his chin, as though it might insulate him from everything going on, just for a while. The house was silent. He'd half expected

Annie to be there, watching him disapprovingly, or clattering around in the kitchen, pointedly making tea. A shame they didn't do ecstasy for ghosts.

Maybe he needed to have nights like that more often – nights where he could let himself go, stop being such an uptight prick. Not that he *was* an uptight prick, of course. But sometimes he knew that that was how other people saw him: calm and assured and controlled. Sensible George. Never doing anything to extremes George. Never letting his hair down George. Uptight, stuffy George.

He thought back to last night and realised he was grinning.

But no: he had to be sensible. He wasn't going to let one spiked drink turn into an addiction, wasn't going to let it take over his life. He was going to be a dad for God's sake. He had no intentions of becoming a junkie dad. He'd had a nice evening, but now it was the next morning and he had a life to get on with. Sometimes sensible George was right.

'Morning,' came a slightly croaky voice.

Leo was standing in the kitchen stretching his arms above his head, looking a bit bleary.

'Sleep well?' he asked George.

'Bloody brilliant!' enthused George before reigning himself back in a bit. 'Yeah, not bad.'

'Tea? No, don't worry – I'll do it. I might be getting on a bit but I reckon I can find everything.'

Leo started shuffling about in the kitchen and George could hear the sound of cups and pots clinking.

'Yeah, thanks,' he said, slightly warily, wondering

whether he really wanted another stranger making himself quite so comfortable in his home. He shook the mean-spirited thought away: Leo was a nice, friendly guy and hadn't they all had the conversation, time and time again, that they all needed to make more friends, interact with the real world, the one outside their door, a bit more? He got up and followed Leo into the kitchen.

'Everyone else still asleep?'

Leo nodded as he filled the kettle.

'Reckon so. Sorry to take your bed.'

George waved vaguely.

'I nearly went in with Mitchell, but I wasn't sure I'd be able to sleep so I thought I'd be better down here.' He paused. 'I think that E must have kept me awake – is that what it does to you?'

'Can do, yeah. You looked like you were having a good time, though,' Leo said. 'Life's too short not to, isn't it?'

George padded over to the fridge to see what breakfast stuff there was, although, curiously, he didn't feel particularly hungry himself. He wondered where Annie was – whether she was sitting in her room, waiting for a suitable moment to come down, all yawns and stretches, pretending she'd been asleep. He yawned. There were some dodgy-looking sausages and two eggs. He shook his head, closed the fridge door and decided to make a start on the washing up.

'Good gig, too,' Leo added as he started to clear the table. 'Been a long time since I saw the guys.'

'You know them?'

A shadow flitted across Leo's face, like someone who'd been caught out. 'Went to a couple of their gigs, years ago. They've not changed much.' He gave an awkward laugh. 'Love to know what their secret is, wouldn't you? Paintings in the attic, maybe. Or drinking the blood of virgins.'

'What?' snapped George, as Leo's comment suddenly brought to mind the three blokes at the gig.

'Virgin blood,' said Leo, pulling a frankly not-very-scary face. 'The new Oil of Ulay – oh, it's Olay or summat now, isn't it?'

'You're asking the wrong person,' George said, still thinking about the vampires that Mitchell had seen off. 'More Annie's territory.'

'She's a great lass, isn't she?' Leo said.

'Yeah,' agreed George, pushing away thoughts of the night before. 'Don't know what we'd do without her.'

'Surprised neither of you have made a move on her.'

George laughed. 'Annie's not like that. And I'm having a bit of a break from women at the moment.'

'Yeah? How come?'

George didn't really want to get into the whole Nina thing. 'Oh, you know...'

He turned at the sound of footsteps on the stairs. It was Annie.

'Morning,' he said.

Leo gave her a wink and she wandered through into the lounge. George dried his hands on the tea towel, the washing up half done, and followed her through.

'Um... Annie... How much of a fool did I make of myself last night?' he asked.

'You were lovely,' Annie replied with a genuine smile that made him feel a bit better.

'You sure? I didn't get too huggy or anything?'

'Actually, I expected you to get huggier – especially with all the baby-love in the air. How were the prospective mums?'

'They were fine. I think they were a bit too wrapped up in themselves – felt a bit like I was crashing their party.'

George sat down on the sofa, alongside Annie.

'Maybe that's something you need to chat to them about,' Annie said. George could see how awkward she was, just making the suggestion. 'You all need to know where you stand, going into this.'

'Yeah,' George said thoughtfully. 'Probably. I'm seeing them later anyway – got the doctor's appointment.'

'Well that's something.' She glanced meaningfully towards where Leo could be heard, singing – quite tunefully – along with Bowie's 'Ashes To Ashes' on the radio. 'You'll know, one way or the other.'

George fiddled with his fingers in his lap and looked up at her a bit sheepishly. 'I've been a bit of a knob, haven't I?'

'Any particular examples of knobbishness?'

'You know what I mean.'

'We've all been a bit knobbish.' Annie put her hand on his knee. 'We could have been a bit more sensitive, though.' She took a deep breath and shook her head.

'You'd think we'd have more to worry about, wouldn't you?'

Leo stuck his head around the corner. 'Tea, Annie? Or coffee?'

Annie shook her head. 'Nothing for me, thanks.'

'Coffee for me,' added Mitchell, jumping down the last two steps into the kitchen. 'Morning, everybody. Sleep well?'

'Took me a while to get off, but yeah,' George said.

'That'll be the drugs,' Mitchell said with a wink, fishing in his jacket pocket for his ciggies. He offered Leo one, but he refused.

'Bad for my health,' he said.

Mitchell came through into the lounge, silently pointing behind him at Leo and raising his eyebrows.

'He's nice,' Annie said quietly. 'Can we keep him?'

'Only if you promise to feed him and empty out the litter tray,' Mitchell said, lighting up. Compared to Kaz's disgusting rollies, Mitchell's normal cigarettes were a breath of fresh air.

'So kiddies, what's the plan for today?'

'George has got his doctor's appointment,' Annie said. 'You in work?'

'Not till this afternoon,' Mitchell said. 'Thought I might have an exciting morning with the telly. What about you?'

'Oh,' said Annie airily. 'Thought I might pop into town and buy a new outfit. Lunch with the girls – cocktails at The Square, you know.'

'Nice,' said George. 'You should look for a grey cardie. You'd look good in a grey cardie.'

'You think?' Annie pulled a face. 'I was thinking of going for a new look. Beige, maybe. Or taupe.'

'What *is* taupe, anyway?' asked Mitchell.

'This,' said Annie, plucking at her cardigan. 'Very practical. A girl could wear this her whole life and never be out of fashion.'

'Good job, then,' George said under his breath as Leo brought in a tray with mugs and the sugar bowl and set it down on the coffee table. 'And what about you, Leo? What's life got in store for you today?'

Leo flopped into the armchair – almost as if he lived there, thought George, stomping down on the teensy bit of irritation he felt.

'Not sure – got a few DVDs back at the flat I thought I might watch. Maybe a trip to the job centre. Living the high life!' He eyed up Mitchell's ciggie. 'Oh, go on then!' he said – and Mitchell tossed him the packet and the lighter.

'You sure?' Annie said.

'One's not going to kill me,' he said.

'If you'd seen some of the sights we've seen, up at the hospital,' said George, having to restrain himself from wagging a finger, 'you wouldn't be saying that.' Annie elbowed him in the ribs. 'What?' he asked.

'It's OK, Annie,' Leo said, and looked at George. 'I've got cancer,' he said.

'Oh,' said George. 'God. I'm sorry. Shit.'

'Yeah,' said Leo, lighting up. 'A bit.'

'God,' said George again.

'Honestly, it's OK,' Leo said. 'We've all gotta go, haven't we?'

George tried hard not to look at Annie or Mitchell. An awkward silence fell.

Annie broke it by standing up suddenly. 'Shopping!' she said brightly.

'You were serious about all that?' asked Mitchell.

'Not really – but we need some milk.'

George frowned, awkward about what he could say in front of Leo. 'You… you all right? About going out, I mean?'

'Can't stay in here all day, can I?'

'I never asked what you do, Annie,' said Leo. 'You work, or what?'

'I'm a full-time housekeeper to these two,' she answered quickly. 'Someone's got to be.'

'And I'm doing a few hours at work before my doctor's appointment,' George said, knocking back the rest of his still-hot tea. The atmosphere suddenly seemed odd, oppressive. He couldn't work out why.

As he faffed around with his jacket in the kitchen, Annie came through. 'You OK?' he asked. 'What's all this "going to get milk" business? Planning on freaking out the man in the corner shop with floating cartons?'

Annie rolled her eyes. 'Leo can still see me, so that's got to be a good thing, hasn't it? Maybe it's an omen – maybe things are finally going right for us all. Last night was great, wasn't it? Well, apart from the drugs thing. And the vampires. And the arguments.' She pulled a lame face. 'Anyway, you're gonna be a dad and that's *got* to be a good thing! Come on, I'll walk as far as the shop with you – see if I feel like the Invisible Woman or not.'

They said their goodbyes to Mitchell and Leo – both of them lighting up more ciggies – and headed out.

As the door closed behind them and they headed down Victoria Terrace, George made a little growling noise.

'I feel such an idiot,' he said. 'About Leo. Why didn't anyone tell me?'

'Didn't think,' Annie said, hugging herself tight as a crisp, autumnal squall sprang up around them, whirling the leaves into mini tornados. There was something refreshing and encouraging about the fact that she felt it through her thin cardigan. Not that she was cold – that kind of thing had long since stopped bothering her. But it made her feel anchored, grounded in reality, instead of just some skinny phantom, slipping through the world without really interacting with it. Maybe this was what impending fatherhood was doing to George – making him feel real, not just a freak living in the House of Freaks and having even freakier adventures. Normal. Normality was underrated, she thought.

'Is it serious?'

'Isn't it always?'

'Depends where it is and how quickly you get it diagnosed.'

'He said he thought it was pancreatic but that it was spreading.'

'And we think we've got problems.'

'George,' Annie said pointedly. 'We *have* got problems. They're just *different* problems.'

'Yeah, I s'pose.'

Annie's hair whipped around her face as they reached the shop on the corner, and she tried to tuck it back behind her ears.

'Good luck at the doctor's, anyway,' she said, giving him a hug. 'It'll be fine.'

'Yeah,' said George. 'It'll be fine.'

'We should do it again,' said Leo as he watched Mitchell finish clearing up. 'Last night.'

'Yeah,' agreed Mitchell. 'Haven't been to a gig in years – it was nice to get out. And nice to see George and Annie having a good time, too.'

'You're an odd lot, you three,' Leo said suddenly. There was an edge to his voice that somehow demanded that Mitchell ignore it – as though it were an opening to somewhere Mitchell knew instinctively he didn't want to go.

'What d'you mean?'

'Oh, nothing really – not *bad* odd. Just *odd*. There's George, having a baby with two lezzers; there's Annie with her OCD thing and all the tea-making and a bedroom with just a chair in it, and there's—'

Mitchell felt the hairs prickle up along his arms. 'You've been in Annie's bedroom?'

'Sorry – accident. Got up for a piss in the middle of the night and went in the wrong room.' Leo raised his hands defensively. 'None of my business, mate.' He grinned and Mitchell realised that Leo must have thought that she was sleeping with *him*.

'It's not what it looks like,' Mitchell said.

144

'Seriously, none of my business. Just saying.' He paused. 'And then there's you.'

'Me?'

At the back of his head, alarm bells were ringing. Some distant, tiny voice was screaming at him to get out of this conversation, to change tack, move on to something else. Anything else.

'Good-looking bloke, 30 maybe, but acts older – and knows more about the '80s than any 30-year-old bloke has any right to...' There was a mischievous twinkle in Leo's eye, along with something else, something harder.

'And that's a crime, is it?' Mitchell's mouth was dry. He sat on the arm of the sofa and leaned forwards, trying to work out where this was going.

Leo's faced cracked into an awkward smile – the smile of someone who's been caught out but is intent on bluffing his way through it. The smile of someone who tries it on with your girlfriend and then, when she's gone to the loo, tells you that it was *her* that had come on to *him*.

'God, no,' he said. 'You're getting me all wrong, mate.'

'Am I?' asked Mitchell, an edge creeping into his voice. 'Mate,' he added.

'Sorry, sorry...' Leo shook his head. 'Must be my hangover. Sorry.'

'Don't look like you've got much of a hangover to me.'

Leo patted his belly. 'Years of practice,' he said. 'Takes a lot to get me drunk.' He stopped and levered himself off the sofa, digging in his back pocket. He pulled out his mobile and fiddled with it whilst Mitchell looked on, wondering what was happening.

'Got something to show you,' he said with a sly wink, and handed Mitchell the phone.

It took Mitchell a moment to work out what he was looking at – the lower half of the screen was black, the upper all blurry red and blue swirls of light. The border between them was irregular and blobby.

'I don't get it,' Mitchell said, frowning. 'What is it?'

Leo got up and came over to Mitchell, taking the phone from him.

'Hmmm,' he said. 'Not the best pic. Hang on.' He pressed a few buttons.

'There! That's a better one.'

Mitchell looked again, and this time it was obvious what he was looking at: it was a picture of the stage at the Bite Me! gig the night before. The dark areas were the crowd, shot from behind; the light areas were the stage.

'Not bad,' Mitchell said – although, in all honesty, it was a crap picture. Obviously Leo's phone wasn't up to taking decent photos in bad lighting.

'You think? Look,' Leo said, touching the screen. 'Guess who that is? Not a very flattering one of her, is it? Bit… grey.'

Mitchell squinted – he could make out a silhouetted figure, arms raised in the air.

'Annie?'

Leo nodded. 'And see that – right next to her…'

Mitchell felt sick. Genuinely, gut-twistingly sick.

'Uh...'

'There,' prompted Leo, tapping the screen.

'You've lost me,' Mitchell said from a million miles away. He could feel his heart thumping in his ears, almost enough to drown out the tiny laugh that Leo gave.

'Yeah, think I did, didn't I? Odd, that, don't you think? Cos I was sure when I took the pic that you were standing right next to her. But look...' He held up the phone, drawing Mitchell's attention to the screen. 'There's no one there – just a gap between her and whoever that skinhead bloke was.' He looked up at Mitchell. 'Weird, eh?'

'Yeah,' said Mitchell. His own voice sounded like someone in another room. Another city. A tiny, lost voice calling from the other side of the world.

'These camera phones, though,' Leo laughed. 'They're crap, aren't they? Can't tell what anything is half the time. And maybe you'd gone to the loo or bent down to tie your shoelace or summat. That'll be it.'

Mitchell smiled tightly and stared away across the room. For some reason he noticed George's CDs, all lined up neatly next to the hi-fi. In alphabetical order.

'Oh, hang on,' said Leo. 'Here's another one...' He paused for a moment. 'That's weird. Look...'

'Leo,' said Mitchell quietly.

'No, look – you're not on that one either, and I could have sworn—'

'Leo, what's going on here?'

Leo looked up, all wide-eyed and innocent. He slipped the phone back into his pocket.

'Sorry, Mitchell – lost me there. What d'you mean?'

Mitchell's voice was low and level. He stood up and looked down at Leo.

'What's this about?'

Leo leaned back in the chair and gave an innocent shrug.

'Nowt, mate, really. Just a bit weird, isn't it, that you aren't on any of those pics – when I could have sworn that you were standing right there in front of me when I was taking them.' He looked around the room in an exaggerated sort of way. 'No pictures of you around here either.'

'And what's that supposed to prove? That I don't like having my photo taken? Since when was that a crime?'

'Fair dos,' said Leo, reaching back into his pocket for his phone. 'Be nice to have one of you, though – a keepsake sort of thing.'

'No,' Mitchell said. This – whatever *this* was – had gone far enough. He wanted Leo out. Out of the house, out of his life. Just *out*.

Slowly, Leo pulled his hand out. No camera.

'I know, Mitchell,' he said, very carefully, very precisely.

'And what is it you think you know, exactly?'

Leo looked up at him.

'I know you're a vampire. Put the kettle on. I think we should talk.'

Chapter
EIGHT

'Good morning, Mr Sands.'

George turned suddenly, his trousers halfway down his legs, his back to the door. Not the kind of position you really wanted to be in when Doctor Declan McGough, the hospital's new administrator decided to strike up a conversation.

'Morning,' blustered George, tugging his trousers back up and almost falling over in the process.

'My apologies.' McGough looked him up and down, a thin smile on his lips. Just for a moment.

George was thrown – partly by the fact that McGough was actually talking to him, not simply addressing him as part of a crowd or a 'strategy meeting'; but mainly by the fact that McGough actually knew his name, a new development since their only previous encounter.

He was an odd one: not a vampire – unless he was some new type that positively relished having his photograph taken. Whenever there had been a photo opportunity at the hospital, there McGough was, polished and immaculate. But there was still something about him that didn't sit right. There was something *too* polished, *too* thoughtful about the way the man presented himself. He was, at a guess, in his fifties. He dressed like a man in his fifties, with a penchant for tweed and smart shirts. And he *acted* like a man in his fifties – a man that had been to a 'good school' and had made steady, if unspectacular, progress up the greasy career ladder ever since. The term 'administrator' could have been coined for a man like him: they couldn't quite work out what it was he did, other than *administrate*. There had been talk of cuts and redundancies when he'd first arrived, but nothing much had come of it and, as far as George and Mitchell could see, he didn't do anything that hadn't been done before. It was just that he did it so well that no one could doubt it was essential to the well-being of the hospital.

And here he was, standing in the door of the orderlies' changing room, hands clasped primly in front of him, saying good morning to a half-naked orderly.

'Morning,' George replied, zipping up his trousers.

'How are things with you, Mr Sands?'

'Um, fine,' said George, feeling like he hadn't quite got the gist of this particular conversation. Was there something he'd done? Was this just the polite, official preamble to a telling-off – or a sacking? No, Guffy – as he was known behind his back – wouldn't have chosen so unofficial a way to do that. He'd have issued a memo – or a series of memos. He'd have timetabled meetings. He'd have commissioned reports and done time-and-motion studies. There'd be graphs and charts and PowerPoint presentations with bullet points. He wouldn't just turn up to stare at George with his trousers down.

A sharp, practised smile cracked his face.

'Good, good. Glad to hear it. Just thought I'd "check in with you", as they say nowadays. Too easy to lose touch, isn't it, in a structure as sprawling and magnificent as the National Health Service?' Guffy took in a perfectly measured breath and let it out. 'And as someone on the front line, so to speak, it's people like you who should be listened to more, isn't it?'

'Is it?'

Guffy nodded firmly. 'Most definitely. It can't have escaped your notice that there are a lot of changes afoot in the National Health Service at the moment. These are difficult times. Lean times. And it's important for me, as Head Administrator, to know how things are.'

George wondered for a moment if Guffy had ever attended a military academy. He could imagine that. All campaigns and precision timing and rations. And he was very fond of military metaphors and similes.

'Things are… good,' George said. He instantly felt stupid. *Good*?

'Pleased to hear it. And how are things with Mr Mitchell? I understand that you two are housemates.'

'He's...' *Don't say "good". Don't say "good".* 'He's fine.' *Damn.*

'Well,' said Guffy, unclasping his hands. 'I'm glad we've had this little chat. Remember, my door is always open if you feel the need to talk about anything. I like to think of myself as "accessible". Important to keep the lines of communication open, don't you think?'

'Definitely,' agreed George, wishing the bloody man would just bugger off and let him get changed in peace.

'Have a good day, then,' Guffy said with a little tip of the head. 'Oh, and while I'm here...'

Here it comes, thought George. *Here comes the sacking...*

'I just wanted to mention the, ah, *pitfalls* of relationships between co-workers. The last thing we want is, say, a promising staff nurse, well liked by colleagues and patients alike – who simply hands in her notice.'

George hadn't been expecting that. Did Guffy know *everything* about him? First Mitchell, now Nina...

'Um, well, Nina and me, we, um...'

'Nina, yes,' Guffy said with exaggerated concern. 'Very worrying. I understand that you and she were "romantically involved". Was she unhappy in her work, may I ask?'

'She had, erm, personal issues.' George was still thrown by all this: how did Guffy know about this? Was it just idle hospital gossip, or did he have a great thick file on George bursting with information about him?

'Really?' Guffy shook his head sorrowfully. 'Such a shame she didn't come to me. There might have been something I could have done – reassured her, helped her out.' He looked straight into George's eyes. 'I do hope, if ever there are "personal issues" giving you concern, that you will feel able to speak to me about them, Mr Sands. Whilst, obviously, our relationship is a work one, I like to think that I'm approachable. We're all one big family here, aren't we, really?'

George nodded.

'Although obviously,' Guffy added, 'we wouldn't want to take that metaphor *too* far, would we? Important to keep clear blue water between work and pleasure, don't you think?'

George could only nod, still trying to process what Guffy had said.

A tight, official smile sprang up on Guffy's face. 'Good. Good. Glad we had this little chat. Nice to "touch base" with you, Mr Sands. My door is always open.' And with that he was gone.

What the hell was that about? thought George as he watched the man go, wondering if he'd missed something. Had there been some sort of secret message in all that? He replayed it in his head, looking for concealed code words like 'redundancies' or 'taking liberties'. Did Guffy know about the room down in the basement? George's 'special room' where he went, every full moon, when his condition got the better of him. Had Guffy found out about that somehow? Was that what he'd meant by 'his door was always open' and 'personal issues'?

No, thought George. No, it couldn't be that. He started to undress again, this time facing the door so Guffy couldn't sneak back and catch him unawares again. If he knew about that he'd have said something straight out. He wasn't the kind of man to fanny around.

But as he finished changing into his scrubs and closed his locker, George realised that he didn't really know what kind of man Guffy was at all.

And that, more than anything, was what scared him.

McGough strode purposefully through the sanitised shabbiness of his hospital, trying not to look down at the scuffed lino or to catch sight of the occasional broken light-fitting. But avoiding looking at those only brought his eyes into contact with chipped paintwork and oh-so-slightly askew pictures on the walls. He was all for art, but, really – some of these... *scrawls*... They weren't art – they were the result of someone 'making artwork'. Some sort of outreach thing to bring 'the community' into his hospital. He shuddered. A hospital was a place of diseases and cures, not a gallery for inept foundation-degree students or idlers with nothing more to do of an afternoon than to watch *Loose Women* and tell themselves that they could be the next John Barrowman. He blamed Nancy Kominsky – that was when the rot had set in. He'd have to have a word with Janice Prescott, head of Human Resources. See if she couldn't have a word with someone. Do something. She was always 'talking the talk' as they said. Time to see if she could 'walk the walk'.

And of course there was the removal of the brand-new yet apparently faulty CCTV to sort out.

He sighed. No one realised quite what a heavy burden fell on the shoulders of a Hospital Administrator. Sometimes he wondered if he wasn't fighting a losing battle against the forces of darkness that constantly nibbled away at it all. A bit of discipline, a bit of order – that was all that was needed. Which reminded him: he had to get Maureen to schedule an appointment with that chap that had emailed him. Professor Jago or something.

Fishing out a notebook and pen, he scribbled a note to himself.

George was still mulling his encounter with Guffy over as he went down to reception to collect some records that had been taxied in from 'The Min' – the rheumatic diseases hospital in Bath. Some old dear had come in for an operation only to discover that they hadn't sent her records down, so she'd been waiting for three hours whilst everyone ran round like headless chickens, trying to find them.

'You OK?'

It was Sarah, on duty on reception.

'Sorry?' said George, staring down at the brown sheaf of notes in his hand.

'You look miles away. Anything wrong?'

'Oh, no – sorry. Just…' He paused. 'I had a weird run-in with Guffy earlier.'

'Run-in?' Sarah looked alarmed.

'Nothing like that – just… I dunno, weird. Cornered me in the changing room and asked if everything was OK.'

'And is it?'

'Couldn't be better.' A grin suddenly broke out on George's face. 'Don't tell anyone…' He looked around to make sure no one was listening. 'But I'm going to be a dad.'

Sarah's mouth literally fell open.

'Bloody hell, George, you kept that quiet! You dirty old dog! Didn't even know you were seeing anyone. I'll be having words with Mitchell when I see him – *I'm* the one that's supposed to be first with the gossip round here. It's in my contract.'

'Noooo,' said George, suddenly a bit bashful. 'It's not like that. Two friends of mine are having a baby and I'm going to be the dad.'

'You mean Kaz and Gail?'

It was George's turn to look astonished. 'You know?'

'Well until you mentioned it I didn't know it was *you*,' Sarah said. 'But Kaz hardly made a secret of the fact that they wanted to have a baby. And putting two and two together… But congratulations anyway.' She leaned over the desk and gave him a kiss on the cheek. 'You'll make a great dad.'

'You reckon?'

'Yeah – course you will. Why? You having second thoughts?'

'I've barely had time for first thoughts, never mind second ones. It's a bit scary.'

'Oh, you'll be fine. How hard can wanking into a cup be?'

'Sarah!' George was shocked and looked around again to make sure no one was watching.

'Just make sure,' she said quietly, 'that you wash it out after. Right?'

'That,' said George, 'is gross.'

'It's you that's going to be doing it,' Sarah reminded him. 'Have you picked names yet? Make sure you get a veto on anything Kaz comes up with, or you'll end up with something like *Angel Delight* or *Fairy Five-Toes*.'

'We've still got all those conversations to come. I'm counting on Gail to be the voice of reason.'

Sarah gave him a look. 'Yeah,' she said. 'Good luck with that.'

George headed off with Mrs Tottingham's notes. He hadn't thought too much about the mechanics of the whole father thing. When he'd tried to bring it up with Kaz, she'd just pulled yucky faces and changed the subject. Maybe he should arrange to meet Gail on his own. Everything seemed to be happening so fast. Was this what *proper* impending fatherhood was like, George wondered. Like a great big dog that launches at you unexpectedly when you go round to a friend's house, with a whopping great sloppy pink tongue all over your face and paws the size of hams wrapped around your neck?

He was puzzling over quite what that simile said about himself when he almost ran into Mossy, coming the other way.

'Ah!' said Mossy loudly and grandly. 'Georgio! Just the man!'

'What have I done now?' sighed George, expecting to be told off for not cleaning something properly, or delivering the wrong patient to the wrong department. What was it with everyone today, wanting to talk to him? He hadn't taken the job of orderly so that people could *talk to him*. Quite the reverse.

'It's not what you've done, but what I hope you're *going to do*. Have you spoken to "the husband" recently?' He winked creepily, and George felt a shudder coming on.

'His name's Mitchell,' he said pointedly, eyebrows raised, peering over the top of his glasses, 'he's not my "husband" – or my "wife" come to mention it. And considering we live together it'd be a bit hard *not* to have spoken to him recently, wouldn't it?'

'And he's not mentioned the bowling?'

George shook his head. 'You only asked about it the other day,' he said, recalling some fragments of a conversation about Mitchell not having turned up for a match or something. 'We do have other things to talk about at home.'

'Like who gets to be Arthur and who gets to be Martha tonight, eh, eh?' grinned Mossy and actually – *actually* – elbowed him twice in the side. 'No worries, Georgio. Just that I can't hold his place open for ever. So, basically, there's a vacancy going on the Health Care Assistant team.'

George sighed inwardly – trust Mossy to refer to orderlies as 'Health Care Assistants': what was wrong with 'orderlies'? 'That's nice,' he said.

'And obviously I'm being pestered left, right and centre by people wanting to join – but you're at the top of my list.'

'Am I?'

'You are indeed, Georgio. You are indeed. So...'

'So...?'

Mossy gave him one of those irritating, pally winks.

'So do I take it that you're up for the challenge?'

'Much as it grieves me,' said George, 'on this occasion I think I'm going to have to decline your kind offer.'

Mossy's face fell. And George suspected that, far from being at the top of his list, he was actually quite near the bottom – and that everyone above him had said no too.

But Mossy wasn't quite ready to give in. 'It's a great way of meeting people,' he winked. 'And by people, obviously, I mean *laydeeeeez*.'

'So's spending Saturday night in casualty with a knife in your stomach, but I know which one I'd choose. Now,' he said, ignoring Mossy's disappointed expression. 'There's a lady waiting for her notes. If I don't get them to her soon, they'll be sending her back home without her operation. And she'll go home to her lonely, damp flat and die of hypothermia because her leg didn't work well enough to let her get to the phone to call for help. And it'll all be your fault.'

'Your loss,' said Mossy with a regretful shake of the head and set off down the corridor. 'If you change your mind, though, just come and find me. Oh – by the way. I never knew Mitchell had rock star friends.'

George turned back to Mossy. 'What?'

'The bloke he was chatting to in the canteen yesterday. Thought he looked familiar. Wasn't until I got home that it suddenly came to me.'

'You've lost me. Who are we talking about? Mitchell doesn't have any friends – never mind rock star ones.'

'Leo Willis – used to be the lead singer with Bite Me! Back in the '80s. Pretty sure it was him, anyway.'

Leo?

'You sure?'

'As sure as I can be – let himself go a bit, but then haven't we all?' Mossy laughed and patted his own paunch. 'Think about the bowling, anyway. Be seeing you.' And with that Mossy was through the swing doors and gone. Whistling.

If Mossy hadn't mentioned Leo's name, George would have sworn that he'd got it wrong. Why hadn't Leo – or even Mitchell – mentioned it? You don't take some new friends to a gig by a band you used to be in and not say anything. Perhaps Leo had just been embarrassed about it. Perhaps he didn't want to look show-offy. Or maybe Leo or Mitchell *had* said something and he'd been too drugged up to remember… He'd ask Mitchell when he got home. There might be all sorts of things that his memory had chucked away from last night. The more he thought about it, and the more distance he put between him and last night, the more George thought that, yes, it had all been very nice, thank you very much, and he'd been very, very happy.

But, as his mother had once told him: 'Happiness is overrated.' You could have too much of a good thing.

With a certain sense of relief at the knowledge that he'd arrested his headlong plunge into the world of dope-fiends and crack-whores, George went to deliver Mrs Tottingham's notes and forgot all about it.

'This is mental,' said Mitchell.

'Aren't I the one who should be saying that?'

'I don't know what you're playing at but just get out, Leo. Get out. Now.'

Leo shook his head and, for a moment, Mitchell thought he saw something. Something thin and pale and vulnerable, not the bluff, stereotypical 'northernness' that Leo had shown up to now. What the hell was going on?

'Either you leave,' said Mitchell, doing his best to control his temper, 'or I'll throw you out. You've got five seconds.'

'Hang on...' Leo held his hands up. 'Look, mate, I've gone about this all wrong.'

'Don't you call me "mate",' growled Mitchell. 'Five... Four...'

'Please, please, just hear me out. Five minutes. That's all I want.'

'Three... two...'

'Five minutes, Mitchell. Please. I've screwed this up, I know, but please.'

Leo had actually clasped his hands together in front of him, as if in prayer.

'One.'

Mitchell moved towards Leo, feeling the anger bubbling up inside him like thick, black oil. For a moment he felt the bloodlust – or something very close to it. Leo somehow flickered between being *Leo* and being some faceless, cowering creature, prey to his predator, pulsing with blood and life. Life that was screaming out to be taken.

Mitchell spun around and pushed his balled-up fists against his eyes. *No.* He wasn't going to let this happen. He wasn't going to let his anger at this... this... man push him over the edge. He'd come this far, drinking the flat, lifeless blood from the hospital's blood banks, keeping away from anywhere that he thought he might lose control.

He turned back to Leo.

'Go now,' he said, his jaw clenched, 'and we'll forget all about it.'

'I can't,' said Leo. 'I've spent too long looking for you.'

'What are you on about?'

'I've been looking for you for nearly two years, trying to track you down, travelling across the country.' Leo's words were coming out in a mad tangle and Mitchell couldn't process them – could barely hear them over the rushing of his own blood in his ears.

'Wait wait,' he said, stopping him. 'What d'you mean?'

'I've been trying to find *you* – Mitchell. Mitchell the vampire.'

'I've told you, I'm—'

Leo shook his head. 'You haven't though – that's the one thing you haven't told me: that you're *not* a vampire.'

'OK,' said Mitchell through clenched teeth. 'I'm not a vampire.'

Leo shook his head, the hint of a manic gleam in his eyes. 'You're lying, and we both know it. And trust me, I know quite a lot about you.'

Mitchell's mind was reeling – were there people out there talking about him? Talking about how long he'd been a vampire? Was there some sort of dossier on him, doing the rounds? Did you just have to type 'vampire, Bristol' into Google and a webpage would come up with his entire life history? Maybe Leo had spoken to Herrick or one of his minions, through the network that had so recently collapsed around them all. Maybe *they* had put Leo onto him. But why *him*? And why come to him like this? That's not what his lot did.

'Look,' Leo was saying. 'It's a lot to take in. I'm sorry, I'm sorry… It's just not the easiest of things to come out and say, all right? But it's not what—'

They both looked up at the sound of the door opening. It was Annie.

'No milk,' she called out wearily, closing the door behind her. 'It'll have to be black for now, unless you can live with UHT. Think there's a carton in the…'

She looked at them as she wandered into the lounge. 'Should I…?' She gestured with her head towards the door. Obviously realising from their faces that she'd come in right in the middle of something.

'Leo was just going,' said Mitchell – suddenly relieved.

He looked at Leo, sitting there, his eyes still glistening.

With a deep breath, Leo got up. Saying nothing, he picked up his jacket and put it on.

'Thanks for last night,' Leo said to Annie who smiled awkwardly.

He turned back to Mitchell and offered him something from his inside pocket: a business card, like the ones you get printed in those machines in shopping centres. It had his phone number and address on it and the name *Leo Willis* in blood-red lettering.

'Call me,' Leo said simply. 'Please.'

And then he was gone.

'Did I just come in at the right time?' asked Annie as the door closed behind Leo, letting in a chilly gust of autumn. 'Or the wrong time?'

'He knows,' said Mitchell, suddenly pacing in the lounge.

'Whoa – calm down, Mitchell.' Annie folded her arms. 'Knows what?'

Mitchell looked up at her, eyes blazing. 'He knows that I'm a vampire. He *knows!*'

'What? I mean how?'

He didn't answer. Annie was almost lost for words. She hadn't seen Mitchell like this for a long time.

'Right,' she said, rushing to the kettle automatically. 'Tea. Sit down. Talk.' Each was punctuated with a firm hand-chop in the air.

'Sod the tea,' Mitchell shouted. Suddenly he was there, right next to her, right in her face. This time, though, his voice was more controlled and measured. And infinitely more scary. 'Leo knows that I'm a vampire. He says he's known for ages.'

'How did he find out?'

'God knows – but he has. He's been chasing me for some reason. *Me*. What's that all about?'

'You know more than me. Mitchell, just sit down and tell me. I've only been gone ten minutes – what happened after I was gone?'

But Mitchell was in no mood to sit down. He started circling around the kitchen table, reminding Annie more of a trapped animal than a human being. There was something eerie about it – a sort of feline grace, a trapped energy that was building up and up. Annie just wanted it defused before Mitchell blew.

'Mitchell, stop this – you're scaring me.'

He looked up at her sharply again, as if to say *You think* you're *scared?*

'Just come and sit down.' Annie reached out to tug at his elbow but he pulled back from her.

'Fine,' she said. 'I'm going in the lounge – you can either shout at me from here or come and sit down and talk to me properly. I think I know which one the neighbours would prefer.'

Mitchell followed her in but refused to sit.

'OK,' Annie said. 'Start at the beginning.'

'He pulled out his mobile and showed me a picture he'd taken last night.'

'Of you?'

'Well, obviously *not* of me – just you, with no one standing next to you. Then he started pissing around, saying "Maybe it was the camera" – but the bastard knew it wasn't. And then he threatened to take one of me there and then.'

'And what did you do?'

'What could I do? I started asking him what he was doing, what it was all about, yeah? And he comes out with it – "I know you're a vampire". My favourite five words in the English language. Jesus!'

With this, Mitchell threw himself into the armchair and then leaned forward, his head in his hands.

'Hang on, hang on,' said Annie, trying to calm everything down a bit. 'So he knows you're a vampire… What if *he's* a vampire? What if that's all this was about – a courtesy call from a new, um, kid in town?'

Mitchell shook his head without looking up.

'We don't do that,' he said. 'That's not the way we do things.'

'What's with the "we"? I thought there was no more "we" any more, not since… Herrick. Who's to say all the old rules or whatever code of conduct thing you lot had going on still applies now? You've said it yourself, Mitchell: it's the storm before the calm. Something's going on out there. Maybe this is just a part of it – mavericks or something. Jumped up little nobodies wanting to wee on your bit of turf.'

'No, no,' Mitchell seemed certain. 'I didn't get that from him. I can smell them, you know? Taste the air around them. There was nothing like that about him. I'd know. Trust me, Annie.'

'OK,' said Annie calmly, for once ignoring the kettle as it clicked off. 'So he's not a vampire, then. Does that automatically make it bad that he knows you're one?'

'Too right it does,' Mitchell said, coming to the boil again. 'Don't care who or what he is, if he knows, then I'm at risk. And if I'm at risk, you two are. Damn.' He slapped his fist into his palm. 'Just when we thought things were calming down a bit, this happens. And after last night...'

Annie pointed to the card that Leo had left and that Mitchell had placed on the arm of the chair.

'Only one way to find out,' she said, gesturing to it with her eyes.

'That's what he wants. That's why he's left it.'

'Doesn't automatically make it bad though. Call him – ask him why he's come looking for you. You can't just leave it like this, Mitchell.'

'I'm not calling him, Annie. I'm not playing his game.'

'Maybe *this* is his game – look at you, Mitchell: you're all screwed up over this. Maybe *this* is what he wants – you falling to pieces.'

Mitchell locked his fingers together and rested his chin on them.

'Maybe...' he whispered.

Chapter
NINE

'Clean pants on?' said Kaz, looking George up and down and brushing a speck of imaginary dirt off of his shoulder.

'Yes,' said George, feeling – and probably looking – for all the world like a little kid on his first morning at 'big school'. They were standing in Pembroke Road, right outside the offices of Doctor Hardimann. Gail slapped Kaz's flapping hands down.

'He's a grown man, Kaz – he doesn't need you fannying around like a mother hen. We'll be getting more than enough of that when Junior's born. I can do without it now, and I bet George could too.'

George smiled a thanks at her and she winked back.

'We need to create the right aura,' Kaz protested. 'The right vibe. He might be a *conventional* doctor –'

she said the word like she might have said 'sexist' or 'racist' '– but he's a highly rated, very expensive conventional doctor, and some of them, yeah, pick up on the vibes of their patients.'

'I'm not a patient,' said George tiredly.

'Whatever,' Kaz said. 'Positive energy, yeah? That's what we want – clean bill of health.' She looked at them both and they nodded, slightly tiredly.

They'd almost been late for the appointment cos Kaz had lost her keys and phone at home somewhere. The keys weren't so much of a problem, but she started fretting that Emilia, her 'healer' wouldn't be able to get in touch with her: she'd fixed up an appointment for George with her too.

George, however, in an uncharacteristic burst of firmness had said 'No'. There had followed twenty minutes of arguments and New Age hippy shit and an almost tearful tantrum, until Gail had stepped in, told Kaz to shut her mouth and reminded her that if she scared George away she'd be lucky to *ever* be a mother.

Somewhat chastened, Kaz had gone quiet on the matter – but only after extracting a promise from Gail that *she* would go and see Emilia.

George hadn't expected to be quite this nervous. The leaflet Kaz had brought for him made it clear that it would just be a standard health check with – because of the baby thing – a few extra tests on fertility, sperm motility and the like. He intended insisting on talking to Doctor Hardimann on his own for a while, during which he'd bring up the subject of hereditary illnesses.

There was no need for Kaz or Gail to know. Ignorance was bliss. Or something.

'Right,' Gail said, checking her watch. 'In we go.'

The building was an ornate Victorian confection of red brick with yellow detailing around the doors and windows and a grand sweep of marble steps up to the front door. George was glad that Gail and Kaz were paying for the consultation. They'd been very tight-lipped about how much it had cost and where the money had come from, but Kaz had let it slip that Gail's parents – who owned a graphic design business in Coventry – were doing quite well for themselves, and had agreed to help out. He didn't feel too bad – especially considering the money he was saving them on private IVF treatment.

A bright, young receptionist took their details, gave George an eight-page questionnaire to fill in, offered them coffee and told them that Doctor Hardimann would be with them soon. She must have been good, thought George: she didn't stare at Kaz's fuzzy braids once.

'Hope you're not planning to get him to deliver the baby too,' George said to Gail in a whisper. 'Unless your parents fancy bankruptcy. Did you get the paddling pools?'

Gail pulled a mock-sad face. 'They were all out.'

'Shame,' grinned George.

'I'm not sure you two are taking this seriously,' Kaz hissed.

'You don't think that it could be you who's taking it *too* seriously?' countered George.

'This is a human life, yeah?' she said, making George want to giggle, 'and no, actually, George, I don't think I *am* taking it too seriously.' She glared past him at Gail. 'And you can stop laughing too!'

The receptionist – thankfully – appeared in front of them as if by magic.

'Doctor Hardimann is ready to see you now. If you'd like to come this way…'

They followed her through an impressive set of double doors, down a corridor that was wider than George's house, to another set of double doors. The receptionist knocked, opened the doors and let them in.

'I can see where your parents' money's going,' George whispered.

It was impressive to say the least: burgundy carpet, white walls, more period detailing than George had seen before – and he'd watched *Upstairs, Downstairs*.

And a chandelier!

'If we slipped him an extra fiver, d'you think I could give birth in here?' Gail murmured to George as Doctor Hardimann stood to greet them.

If the building was impressive, Doctor Hardimann himself was a little less so. In fact, if George hadn't known better, he might have assumed he was a medical student on placement. He looked like he was a way off his thirtieth birthday – thin with a crown of blond hair and a ruddy complexion. But at least he had a smart suit on: in a doctor's lab coat he'd have looked like the YTS scientist who only got to heat safe things in test tubes. He looked slightly nervous as his eyes scanned the three of them. They all shook hands and he invited them to sit down.

He ran through the basics – names, ages, reasons for their 'arrangement'. Fortunately, Gail did most of the talking on behalf of the two women. Kaz seemed a bit overawed by it all. George was relieved – he'd expected to have to send her out whilst he and Gail spoke to the doctor, but she was on her best behaviour. When all the 'joint' discussions were over, Doctor Hardimann asked Gail and Kaz to leave whilst George got his 'go'.

The receptionist brought him a cup of coffee and whilst he drank it, Hardimann went through the questionnaire.

'Well,' he said brightly. 'How are you feeling about impending fatherhood?'

'Good, good,' said George, not quite sure what an appropriate response would be. He didn't want to appear too laid back, or the doctor might think he wasn't serious; and over-enthusiasm might look, well, a bit creepy. 'I'm feeling good.'

'So… perhaps you'd like to tell me why you've decided to go down this route, with Gail – and, erm, Kaz.'

'They asked,' said George simply – and then realised that this might sound a bit half-hearted. 'And it seemed like a good idea.'

Hardimann nodded and scribbled something. What could he be scribbling? 'Easily led'?

'That's very…' George expected him to say 'public-spirited' '…thoughtful of you. Now, I see here that you were keen to talk about the possibility of hereditary diseases. Is there any particular reason for that?'

Yes, thought George. *I'm a werewolf.*

'No,' he said. 'Not really. Well…' Hardimann raised an encouraging eyebrow. 'I had a great grandmother who had, um, something.'

'Something?'

George shuffled in his seat. He hadn't really thought this through, had he? He'd expected just to be able to bluff his way through on the basis of having a slightly odd great grandmother who might – or might not – have had some vague, descriptionless illness.

'She used to have mood swings.'

'Mood swings.'

George nodded. 'Quite bad ones. From what I hear.'

'And was there any suggestion of what the cause might have been? Was she on any medication? Did she consult a doctor? If so, we might be able to track down her records.'

'No, no,' George said. 'She lived in Wales.'

'They do have doctors in Wales,' Hardimann pointed out. 'And the National Health Service. What was her name?'

'Bertha,' said George without hesitation. He had no idea what this particular fictional great grandmother's name was – well, not until now. Wasn't a very Welsh name, though, was it?

'And her last name?'

'Mitchell,' said George. It wasn't like Bertha Mitchell actually existed, so he wasn't going to make things worse by giving her a fictional name, was he?

Hardimann scribbled. 'I'll need some more information – where in Wales did she live? And if you have her birth date – or even the date of her death – it might help to track down her records.'

George just gawped.

'Bangor,' he said. The first Welsh place that came into his head. Probably because it always sounded a bit rude. 'No idea about the dates, though. Sorry.'

'Not to worry,' Hardimann said. It was clear from his face that he didn't think this was going to be a productive route to take. 'And you have concerns that this illness of hers – the mood swings – might be hereditary? What about your parents and grandparents?'

'No,' said George. 'I mean, I don't think so.' *Oh God, what had he been thinking of? Why had he thought that lying was the thing to do? He'd never been good at lying. They'd check with his mother and find out it'd all been lies and that he'd never had a great grandmother called Bertha Mitchell who never lived in Bangor, and he'd be done for perjury or perverting justice or something…*

George realised that Hardimann was staring at him expectantly.

'Sorry?'

'Your parents and grandparents.'

'Oh. Yes.' George swallowed. 'They're fine.'

Hardimann nodded slowly and put down his pen.

'Mr Sands,' he said gently. 'My experience as a doctor has taught me that, quite often, patients come to me with concerns that, for one reason or another, they're not able to voice. Nagging doubts, fears about their own health – quite often their own *sexual* health. Things that perhaps even *they* don't realise that they're worried about.' He paused, pointedly, and looked at George. 'Is there anything else that's bothering you? Perhaps something about the actual *procedure*?'

'Procedure?'

'The insemination.'

'Oh God, no,' George said quickly. 'No problems with that. Not at all. Piece of cake, that.' He laughed – perhaps a bit too loudly – and did a quick hand-wiggling mime.

'Right,' said Hardimann.

Bloody hell, thought George. *I've just mimed masturbating in front of the most expensive doctor in Bristol. After lying to him.*

'Not that that's all there is to it, obviously,' he added hastily. 'There's all the stuff with the turkey baster.'

'Things have moved on a little,' Hardimann said with a tight smile. 'We can supply you with something a little more effective than, as you say, a turkey baster. But the process is similar, yes. Could we just go back to your concerns about having a hereditary illness. Is there anything that makes you think that you have inherited your great grandmother's "mood swings"? Was she your maternal great grandmother or your paternal one?'

'Does it make a difference?'

'It can do – some diseases pass down the female side of the family more readily than the male.'

'Yes,' George said. 'The female side. My mother's grandmother.'

That's OK. It can't get any worse. Mother's side, father's side. You're not going to get in any deeper for that one.

Hardimann made a note. 'So...?'

'Sorry?'

'The mood swings – have you any reason to believe you *have* inherited them? Do you suffer from mood swings?'

'Oh, God, no. Well... Maybe. A bit. Nothing bad. I'm not like an axe murderer or anything.'

Hardimann's smiled tightened another notch. George could almost hear the mechanism in the man's head, whirring and clicking. Fortunately, he didn't make any notes about this latest stupid outburst. George had visions of the police knocking on his door, next time someone was found murdered in Bristol with an axe, asking for Bertha Mitchell's great grandson.

'And you've no other reason to be concerned, other than your great grandmother?'

George shook his head.

'Well,' Hardimann said cheerily, 'I don't think there's anything to worry about. Obviously, we'll do all the appropriate tests and then, when we have the results, we can have another chat and talk things through. It's quite normal to be concerned, Mr Sands. Believe me, you wouldn't be the first person to have worries or doubts. Perhaps that's all these are. It's a big commitment, bringing a child into the world.'

George nodded numbly, realising that, underneath all the excitement and jollity and general whoo-hooness of it all, he hadn't really sat down – on his own, in a quiet room, perhaps with some *Classic FM* on – and thought all this through. Made lists – pros and cons. Maybe given each one a score and then totted up the points.

He looked up at Hardimann – all youth and suit and period detailing, looking back at him expectantly. Had he asked a question? Had last night's drugs addled his brain to such a degree already that he couldn't hold a simple conversation?

Maybe Mitchell had been right – and maybe he just wasn't ready to be a father.

'Any other questions before I put you in the safe hands of Nurse Conway?' He gave an awkward grin. 'Sorry,' he said. 'Just my little joke.'

George tried to smile, but somehow, it just wasn't there.

LAS VEGAS

They say Las Vegas is a different city after dark, but take a cab off the Strip and it's a different world.

Nevada's Finest Little Wedding Chapel shares a parking lot with Nevada's Skankiest Little Whorehouse, and souvenir sellers rub shoulders with drug dealers on every corner. And it's dark; at best poorly lit but more commonly reliant on open curtains and advertising neon to illuminate even sections of the street. Dark figures move round in the shadows and the air is full of little unpleasant sounds – thuds and smacks and groans as the animals kill one another.

I love it here.

I can see her across the road, walking quickly up and down in the thin puddle of light created by a rare flickering street lamp. Younger than I like – 16, maybe 17 at a push – but in this place it's best to aim as young as possible. Lessens the chances of supper turning out to be riddled with disease or dope. Bad meat. She's skinny, as they all are, and she's a cutter. I can smell it from here – and the crusted blood is just enough of a taste to catch the interest of my hunger.

It's like this – when I'm hungriest – that I'm at my best. Powerful, unstoppable. A force of nature. I'm a meteoroid slipping silently through the blackness of space, headed straight for Earth. I'm the car coming up your driveway with its headlights off and no sign of who's behind the wheel.

I cross the road.

I've seen so many kills over the years. From the most basic grab-and-bite to the literally insanely complex. Even I had nightmares for a while after an evening in the early 1940s with a soldier who bound his victims so tightly in wire mesh that small polyps of flesh popped through every tiny gap; polyps which could be razored off and then sucked like a bloody lozenge. Freaky bastard.

Me, though, I fall somewhere between those two extremes, in an area where invention and flair carry more weight than either speed or sadism. Which is just a pompous way of saying that I take my time but I'm not a nutter. Ma always told me not to gulp my food.

Sometimes it's more of a frenzy.

I come up behind her, three quick steps out of the darkness. One hand clamps round her mouth as I slide the nails of the other across her cheek. The skin peels back in a short line, and curls back in on itself like a roller blind. The blood wells up sluggishly along the cut and slides down her cheek. I lick from her jawbone to the corner of her eye, slowly, deliberately, with the full width of my tongue.

It's enough.

And sometimes it's all about the frenzy.

I bite her hard, my teeth bursting through her skin like fingers popping through cellophane. I press the whole of my face into the wound, the slippery raw flesh pressing against either cheek as I feed. It's uncontrollable gluttony, like sex, like murder.

Eventually I slide down the alley wall, her still twitching body on top of me, her chin resting on my cheek and blood pulsing slowly and thickly from the remains of her neck. I lie there, replete and supine, lazily contented with my mouth slackly open and the blood washing over my lips.

Viva Las Vegas!

Chapter
TEN

Mitchell heard her before he saw her. And he smelled her even before that. A heady, poisonous odour of perfume, arrogance and blood. He hadn't noticed the perfume last night. Maybe she'd been dressing down. Maybe she'd put it on specially for him.

He was standing on the top of the very same car park he'd been in recently with Ivan and Daisy. What was it with vampires and car parks? Too many bad vampire movies probably.

Evening had fallen over Bristol, and without the autumn sun it was just another wet and windy city. Down below, traffic streamed through the city's veins and arteries. That's how Mitchell saw the place. Was that a vampire thing, too? Did everything come down to blood? Had he actually put as much distance between himself and the others as he liked to think?

Her heels clicked on the damp concrete and came to a halt.

'Mitchell,' she said precisely.

He turned – and couldn't help but raise an eyebrow.

Olive King – looking even more like a power version of Grace Jones than she had the night before, immaculately turned out in a grey business skirt and jacket, crisp white blouse with a red scarf at her neck, and hair tied back so tightly that it strained her perfect skin almost to tearing point – prowled a little closer.

'Is your name *really* Olive?' he said. 'I just don't see you as an Olive, I really don't. No one's called Olive nowadays.'

'Fashions change, Mitchell. Names change. Everything changes.'

'Except us.'

'Except us. Time for a new name, then. What d'you think? Keisha? Lianne?' Olive pulled a face. 'A bit common, maybe. Any suggestions?'

'How about Vampyra?'

Olive considered it for a moment, turning and leaning on the concrete wall and staring out of the city with Mitchell.

'I'll add it to the list. I must admit, I didn't expect to hear from you so soon. Isn't it customary to wait for twenty-four hours before calling? Any sooner and you look desperate; any later and you look like you just don't care.' A tiny smiled twitched at the corner of her mouth. 'And I really hope you do care, Mitchell.'

'You knew, didn't you.'

'Sorry?'

'About Leo. That's why you gave me your number. Is that why you were there last night?'

'Aren't we allowed to have a night out without there being a hidden agenda?' Olive pressed her hand to her bosom theatrically.

'There's always a hidden agenda with you lot. So who were the pit bulls last night, then? Toy boys?'

Olive pulled an expression of distaste.

'They're nobodies. Wannabes. But I suppose that's all anyone is at the moment. Wannabes. Problem is, no one knows what they actually *want to be* if you get my meaning. Since Herrick's little... accident, everyone's just running around, trying to work out their place in the scheme of things.' She paused. 'You really should think about coming back, you know. There's a Mitchell-shaped hole at the heart of it all.'

'I wasn't interested before and I'm not interested now.'

Olive let out a gentle, disapproving hiss.

'That's such a shame.'

'Why don't you hammer it into an *Olive*-shaped hole.' He looked at her again. 'I'm sure you wouldn't find it difficult.'

'No matter how I "hammered it", it would never be quite big enough, Mitchell. Trust me. None of this...' She nodded in the direction of the city's lights. 'None of this is quite big enough. Not for me.'

'Delusions of grandeur kicking in already?' asked Mitchell 'You should be careful.'

'Careful of what?'

'Once upon a time,' Mitchell said, as if telling a bedtime story, 'there was a little vampire called Herrick, who wanted to grow up to be a really *big* vampire called Herrick. And we all know what happened there. No happy ever afters. A lesson for us all.'

'In humility?'

'In having dreams.'

'Herrick was a product of his time and place,' Olive said, almost wistfully. 'This place. We're shaped by our environment, the people around us. History. And we have *so much* history, don't we? Right back to 1630, but I don't suppose I need to tell you about that.'

Mitchell knew about Richard Turner, the first vampire in Bristol, the start of it all.

'Sometimes it feels like a tower beneath our feet that we can survey the rest of humanity from,' Olive continued. 'And sometimes it just feels like a weight around our necks. Whichever, it's what makes us.'

'And what has this place made you?'

'Are you expecting me to say "bored"? Or "tired"? No, Mitchell. It's made me *ambitious*. I've seen what happens when you let your vision become too blinkered. Too parochial. "We are all in the gutter, but some of us are looking at the stars".' She smiled. 'Oscar Wilde.'

'*The Portrait of Dorian Gray*?'

'*Lady Windermere's Fan*. And it's "Picture", not "Portrait". A lot of people make that mistake.'

'Well,' said Mitchell. 'When you've lived as long as we have, there's only room up there for so many memories. Eventually it's one in, one out.'

Olive gestured out to the city again. 'That's what they are, isn't it? Our paintings in the attic. Keeping us young whilst they wither and die.'

There was a moment's silence, and then Mitchell turned to her, shaking his head.

'What *is* it with you lot?' he said. 'No wonder they all want us dead. Jesus, even if you weren't a vampire, I think *I'd* want you dead, spouting bollocks like that.'

He caught Olive's eye and she held his gaze for a few seconds.

'Oh,' she said. 'I like you!' And the mask-like beauty of her face cracked into a brilliant grin. 'I like you very much, Mitchell. I can see why they talk about you, I really can.'

It was hard not to smile back: there was something very alluring about Olive King.

'What do you know about Leo?'

Olive raised a single eyebrow.

'Leo Willis,' expanded Mitchell. 'He was with me last night. You know him?'

'Ahh... *that* Leo.'

'You know him?' Mitchell repeated.

'I know *of* him. What's your involvement with him?'

'He's just someone I've met. How do you know him?'

'I'd keep Mr Willis at a distance, Mitchell.'

'You're not answering my question.'

Olive nodded, thoughtfully. 'You're right, I'm not.'

'He's not one of us, is he?'

'You know, I admire your cheek,' Olive said,

sidestepping Mitchell's question again.

'Cheek?'

'You're happy to talk to us when you want something. And you're happy to shun us when you don't. You can't have it both ways. Information costs, Mitchell. Maybe it's time you learned that.'

'And the price would be…?' He laughed. 'Let me guess: come back into the fold, yeah?'

'Is that such a high price? The fringe benefits are enormous, you know.'

'Full healthcare and pension?' Mitchell shook his head. 'Not for me, I'm afraid. Happier as a freelancer. There's always small print in the contract that you don't spot until it's too late, isn't there?'

Olive shrugged. 'Your choice. But be very careful of Mr Willis. That's all. A freebie. For old times' sake.'

Mitchell held her gaze: he knew he'd get nothing more from her, and was lucky to have got as much as he had.

'If you don't mind my saying,' Olive added thoughtfully. 'You're looking a little peaky. Hope you're eating well. A big boy like you needs to keep your strength up. How's the diet going?'

'It's amazing what you can live on if you really try.'

Olive checked her watch. 'Well as long as you're getting your five-a-day…'

She smiled again and turned to leave. She'd gone a couple of paces when she suddenly turned.

'Annie!' she said brightly, looking over her shoulder.

'What about her?' Mitchell tensed up.

'The name. Annie. I like it.' She looked thoughtful for a moment. 'Goodbye Olive, hello Annie. What d'you think? Has a certain ring to it, doesn't it?'

And before Mitchell could answer, Olive had gone, leaving behind the click click click of her heels and the scent of menace and winter.

'I thought we'd have pizza,' said Annie brightly as George closed the door behind him and shook the drizzly rain out of his hair. 'And then I'll tell you about Mitchell and Leo!'

'Fine,' he said, shucked off his coat and padded through into the lounge. 'Whatever.'

Annie followed him through, puzzled. 'Someone's had a bad day – wasn't it your doctor's appointment this afternoon?'

George nodded glumly from the sofa as he pulled off his trainers. He looked over at her.

'Annie, what am I doing?'

He looked suddenly close to tears.

'What?' Annie asked, sitting down on the sofa next to him. 'What's happened?'

'I don't know if I can go through with this.'

'Start at the beginning.'

'I nearly told him,' said George blankly, staring into nowhere.

'Told who what?'

'The doctor. About my... what I am. The werewolf thing.'

Annie's mouth dropped open. 'You didn't, though.'

George shook his head.

'I was *this* close. Thought I could use that doctor-patient confidentiality thing, but then I remembered that it doesn't cover everything. It's not like with a priest. They've got a duty to report anything that could be dangerous to other people. And telling someone that you're a werewolf sort of falls into that category, doesn't it? Especially when you're there cos you're about to donate sperm to a friend to make a baby.'

There was something about the way that George said 'make a baby' that was so endearing. Annie pulled him closer. George let himself be hugged for a few seconds.

'Anyway – what was that about Mitchell and Leo? Good news?'

'No,' Annie said. 'This is bad – really bad.'

'Why? What happened?'

'You know this morning, when we went out? Well when I got back they were in the middle of a right old barney.'

'Why? Thought they were bosom buddies.'

'Uh-uh,' Annie said. 'Leo knows about Mitchell.'

'That he's a…' George's eyes grew.

Annie nodded.

'Bloody hell – and I thought *I'd* had a weird day. What happened? I mean, how?'

Annie shrugged.

'We don't know. Apparently, Leo took photographs at the gig and Mitchell wasn't on them and then this morning he accused him of being a vampire. I came back in – just in time to stop Mitchell killing him, I think. I've not seen him like that for ages.'

George pulled a thoughtful face. 'So Leo – he's not a vampire then? Not one of Mitchell's lot?'

'Mitchell doesn't think so.'

'So what's he playing at?'

Annie shrugged again. 'That's the problem – Mitchell doesn't know.'

'Maybe he's blackmailing him? Oh, that reminds me – hang on.'

George rushed upstairs and came down with his laptop and set it up on the coffee table. He plugged it into the phone socket in the wall and went online.

'Leo,' George said in answer to Annie's unspoken question. 'At work today Mossy said something about him.'

'About Leo? What?'

'That he used to be in Bite Me!'

'The band we saw?'

George nodded as he typed. 'Yes!' he said triumphantly. 'Look!'

Annie peered over George's shoulder – there was a website – a fan site – for Bite Me! with a list of their hits (and an even longer list of non-hits), along with details of the band members. And there was Leo – looking considerably younger and slimmer.

'Well, if nothing else it just goes to show he's not a vampire, doesn't it?' said Annie with some relief. 'Unless he's become one in the past couple of years. God,' she said, leaning further forward to read the page. 'Seriously into his goth stuff, wasn't he?'

'Look,' said George, pointing. 'He fell out with the band...' His voice tailed off. 'Oh my...' he whispered.

Annie read for a few seconds and turned to George. This was bad.

George leaped to his feet and rushed to the phone.

'Call Mitchell,' he said, handing his mobile to her. 'I'm calling the hospital.'

'Why?'

'Just call him – tell him what we've found.'

Annie found Mitchell on speed-dial and pressed the button. All she heard was a message telling her that Mitchell's phone was switched off.

Mitchell checked the name of the building. This was the right place. And boy was it a dump. Which, in Mitchell's opinion, just about summed up the area of St Philips Marsh. It was little more than an industrial area to the east of the city, shabby and rundown and with little more to its credit than a retail park, a bowling alley and a cinema. The lack of people and traffic lent it a deserted, unearthly air, and Mitchell was wondering whether he shouldn't have listened to Olive and stayed away.

But if there was one thing guaranteed to make him do the opposite, it was someone like Olive handing out advice. And no matter what kind of nutter or blackmailer or whatever Leo turned out to be, Mitchell had to face him. If he didn't, if he just let Leo walk out of his life, he'd always be looking over his shoulder. And he'd had a lifetime of that. The fact that Olive had clearly heard of him made him so much more curious. Maybe that had been the point: perhaps Olive had *wanted* him to find Leo. Reverse psychology. But you could play that game for ever, couldn't you? Flipping it backwards and forwards until you were no better off than you'd been at the start.

Two kids came hurtling out of the silence on a bike, one on the seat and one standing behind him. He jumped back just in time and they swore at him and vanished into the dark like rats. Not a good advertisement for humanity, Mitchell thought. Sometimes he could see the vampires' point of view…

He found the entrance to the building and pressed the buzzer for number 26, Leo's flat. There was no sound, no indication that the buzzer even worked. And there was no reply. Damn, what if Leo was out? His mobile! He had the number in his mobile, even though he couldn't find the card that Leo had left. But when he checked it, the battery was dead. *Damn.*

As he turned to leave, he saw movement behind the heavy doors – someone was on their way out. Mitchell spun on his heel and headed towards the door with confidence, hoping to fool whoever was coming out into thinking he lived there too. He needn't have bothered: the woman was too busy lighting up a cigarette to even look at him. He slipped past her and was inside the grubby hallway as the door slammed shut behind him.

The thought of getting stuck in a piss-stinking lift didn't appeal, so he headed on up the stairs, taking them two at a time.

What was he going to say to Leo? What was Leo going to say to *him*? Perhaps he should have gone home, slept on it. But he didn't have the patience. He didn't know what Leo wanted from him – but after the way they'd left it this morning, and after Olive's bloody cryptic remarks, he needed to know now. By the time he'd reached Leo's floor, his heart was thumping in his chest. He paused for a few moments, listening to the sounds of televisions and shouting and music. Ordinary people.

Portraits in the attic.

Mitchell found flat 26 – the letterbox was half hanging off. He listened at the door – silence.

He could still walk away couldn't he? He could still leave Leo to rot in this place, forget he'd ever met him. Of course, he couldn't. If he didn't go through with it, he'd always wonder.

He took a breath and knocked.

Chapter
ELEVEN

When the door opened, Mitchell's first thought was that he'd got the wrong flat: the man who answered bore little resemblance to the Leo he'd seen the night before. He looked unwashed, unshaved. His eyes were half open and bleary. He just stared at Mitchell. The flat stank of damp and weed.

'Mitchell?'

Leo's eyes widened, although Mitchell couldn't work out whether it was fear or just surprise.

'Thought we needed to talk,' Mitchell said.

'Yeah, yeah,' Leo said, backing away from the door.

Mitchell stood there, expectantly, until Leo cottoned on. A vampire had to be invited in.

'Sorry,' he said. 'Come in, come in.'

He stood back to let Mitchell through and closed the door behind him.

The flat was gloomy, the hallway piled up with books and newspapers and junk. Two bin-liners, their necks twisted and tied, stood beside the door, a cardboard box of wine and beer bottles next to them.

'It's that way,' Leo said, gesturing to the end of the corridor.

On the dark blue walls were badly framed posters and prints – movie posters mainly. *The Lost Boys*, *The Hunger*. Mitchell stopped as one particular poster – an ancient-looking green and red one – jumped out at him. *Captain Kronos Vampire Hunter.*

Jesus!

His heart started hammering. What had he got himself into? He watched the sad, shambling figure of Leo turn in the doorway and wait for him, silhouetted in the light from the lounge. Was it a trap? Mitchell glanced back over his shoulder: Leo hadn't locked the door, had he? No, he was pretty sure he hadn't.

He turned back to Leo, who'd moved on into the lounge. What sort of threat was he? A middle-aged, sad old loser with cancer. No vampire hunter, surely. But what did he know? How did you recognise a vampire hunter? He was pretty sure they didn't dress like Peter Cushing and come at you with stakes and holy water. Was that what Olive had meant by 'be careful'? Was this how it was going to end? Staked through the heart in a squalid flat? After all he'd been through, all he'd seen.

Mitchell felt sick. Something whispered at him to back out, to leave now. Suddenly Mitchell saw the appeal of immortality – when you're facing death, anything – *anything* – is better. He remembered when he had first encountered Herrick, in the muddy trenches, corpses around him, the stink of death and waste and hopelessness in his nostrils.

And he'd made a deal with Herrick. Leave Mitchell's men, let them go – and take him instead.

But had that been the *real* deal? Had Mitchell traded his comrades' lives for his own? Or had he just looked into the face of Death and grabbed at his only chance of life? And had he just rewritten his own memories to make himself the hero?

'Come through,' said Leo.

Mitchell walked into the lounge. It was as shabby and down-at-heel as the hallway. Cheap bookcases lined one wall, packed with DVDs and paperbacks and dozens of vinyl albums. A huge flatscreen TV stood in one corner, the picture frozen – a woman standing near a window, holding a glass. The remote control was on the arms of a torn, stained black leather sofa. Mitchell looked around. *The apartment of a serial killer* suddenly sprang into his head from somewhere.

A black ash coffee table was covered with cans and pizza boxes and two overflowing ashtrays. So much for the not smoking, then.

'Drink?' asked Leo, padding through into the kitchen. He wore grey slippers. *Slippers for God's sake. A vampire killer in slippers.*

Mitchell almost laughed at the sheer ridiculousness of it all, but realised that it was just a kind of panic that he was holding down.

'No thanks,' he said.

'Mind if I do?' asked Leo. Without waiting for an answer, he opened the fridge and pulled out a can of beer.

Mitchell wandered over to the bookcase and tipped his head on one side, reading the titles of the DVDs: *Fright Night*, *Dracula 2000*, an *Angel* box set…

This was just madness. What was he doing here? In the flat of *The Little Goth Who Never Grew Up*. He turned sharply as he heard a hiss – half expecting Leo to be there with a crucifix. But he was still in the kitchen, opening his beer.

'What made you come?' asked Leo, gesturing for Mitchell to sit down.

He stayed standing.

'What d'you want from me?' Mitchell asked, trying to keep the fact that he didn't know if he actually wanted to hear the answer out of his voice. 'Kill me? Expose me? Blackmail me? What is all this, Leo?'

Leo shook his head sadly.

'I was about to explain when Annie came in this morning. You look rough. Are you OK, mate?' Leo took a few steps forward, his face looking genuinely concerned. 'You look terrible.'

'How d'you expect me to look?' snapped Mitchell. 'That stunt you pulled this morning…'

'Honestly, I'm sorry – I'm really sorry. I'm not gonna kill you, mate, or blackmail or anything. Why the hell would I do that?'

'Then why the lies? You said you've been tracking me down, following me. What kind of games have you been playing? Getting to know George and Annie, the gig, last night. What's it all about, Leo?'

'If you sit down, Mitchell, I'll tell you.'

'You'll tell me standing up,' Mitchell growled, 'and you'll tell me now, otherwise I'm out that door and you won't see me again. Ever!'

Leo nodded and eased himself down into the sofa.

'OK. Simple as this – I want you to make me a vampire.'

Mitchell suddenly realised that he had no idea how long he'd been staring at Leo for. It felt like for ever.

'You want *what*?' His voice sounded like somebody else's.

'I want you to turn me into one of you.' Leo paused. 'Please.'

And then it all clicked into place.

The cancer. The Big C. That's what Leo wanted – he... Mitchell almost laughed, it was so simple and so obvious. He didn't want to die. Leo was no killer, no threat to Mitchell. He just *didn't want to die.*

A wave of relief rushed over Mitchell, like cold heartburn. How had he not seen it?

Leo was looking at him, eyes wide with expectation. With hope.

'No,' said Mitchell gently.

'What?' Leo looked genuinely confused. 'Why not?'

'Because... because I don't do that any more.'

'What d'you mean, you don't do that any more?'

'Simple.' Mitchell held his hands out, palms up. 'I don't do that.'

'But you're a vampire – that's what you lot *do*.'

'You've picked the wrong one. Sorry. Wasted trip.'

199

Mitchell's legs actually felt shaky. The anticlimax of discovering what Leo wanted was hitting him now. Vampire or no vampire, his body still had the same hormonal surges as any other body. He might be able to control them better, steel himself against their chemical caresses, but they still affected him, etching away at something inside him, making him – what? More human?

'Plenty more of us out there – go find one of them.'

Leo shook his head sharply. 'It has to be you, mate.'

'Why?'

'Cos you're... you're summat special. You're Mitchell.'

'And?'

'It's taken me nearly two years to find you. I'm not just looking for any vampire.'

'What is this? Some sort of fan club?'

'You've got a reputation out there, with the rest of 'em. The rest of your lot. You must know that.'

Mitchell had heard others say that, say that he was 'special', different. But that was just because he refused to join them, refused to play their games. What was Leo on about? Maybe he'd been closer than he thought with the 'fan club' remark: maybe Leo was some weird, sick stalker.

'It has to be you that does it,' Leo said. 'It has to be.'

'Why, though? Why me?'

Leo shook his head. 'You wouldn't understand.'

'Try me.'

'You'd be surprised how much there is out there about you, if you know where to look, who to ask.

What you've done, where you've been. Look!'

Leo suddenly jumped out of his seat and ran around the coffee table, dropping to his knees in front of the book case. He slid open one of the cupboard doors at the bottom and pulled out a huge scrapbook – the kind Mitchell remembered from years ago, purple and pink sugar paper. A bright orange cover. It was bulging. Leo pivoted on his knee and presented it to him, like some trophy. Or an offering to a god.

With a sick curiosity, Mitchell opened the scrapbook: cuttings from newspapers – back as far as – *Jesus!* – 1960. Unexplained deaths. Corpses found with puncture wounds. Missing bodies. Missing *people*. He turned the pages slowly. More and more, gathered from all over Europe – and a couple from the States. He scanned the text, looking for his own name. Nothing. Just talk of vampires, rumours of 'the undead'. Silly stories and clippings about murders, fairy tales and coroners' reports, side-by-side; a ridiculous juxtaposition of the banal and the sickening.

And then there were letters – handwritten letters, letters typed on ancient typewriters with misaligned characters. A couple of telegrams. And then he started to see his own name. Nothing that could get him locked up, nothing as obvious as that. Other people's communications *about* him: 'Mitchell was here last weekend…' (a woman called Grace in Edinburgh); '… spoke to Mitchell about Collinghurst but he claimes to kno nothing…' (a signature that might have been 'Edward' or 'Eduardo'); '… I've been told he's moved on again but no one's seen him…'

'What's this all about?' Mitchell barked, tossing the scrapbook down onto the coffee table. He didn't want to see any more, despite the gruesome fascination of seeing other people talking and writing about him.

Leo opened his mouth, his breath held as he clenched and unclenched his fists; a child with a secret that he was bursting to let out.

'Sorry,' he said eventually. 'I know what it looks like. But honest, it's not.'

'It's not what? Not some sick stalker fantasy?'

'OK, OK – forget all that.' Leo pulled himself up on the sofa. 'I know you're on the wagon, so-to-speak. I know that you've not – what's the phrase you lot use? "Made a killing?" – for a while now. But this is different.'

Mitchell raised a hand to stop him, but Leo ploughed on.

'Hear me out, please, mate. Five minutes. And if you still feel the same, then fair enough. Go home, forget you ever met me.' He stopped, waiting for Mitchell to say something. When he didn't – because, despite everything, Mitchell realised he wanted to hear – he continued.

'The cancer, yeah? It's eating me up. I told Annie that I got the results of the tests yesterday. It's not looking good. They reckon I've got six months maybe. And that's it. End of. No more. Maybe you've forgotten what it's like, mortality. But the rest of us have to live with it. And it's not until you're staring down the barrel of a gun that you realise how much you really, *really* do not want to die.' Leo gestured to the window of the flat where grimy orange curtains hung, framing the night. 'Everyone thinks they're going to live for ever. Doesn't matter how much you tell yourself that one day you're going to die, no one actually *believes* it.' He slapped his hand against his chest. 'Not in here they don't. Not really. Not until summat like this comes up. It's other people that die: old people, sick people, people in car accidents. Not *them*.'

'You think I don't know that?'

'I know you know it. But you're *immortal* for God's sake. You're *a* god! You don't *feel* it, not any more.'

'You don't know what I feel,' Mitchell said flatly.

'No, but I know what you *don't* feel. You don't feel that every day, every minute, you're getting one step closer to death.'

He paused.

'Last night, when you and George and Annie were talking – after I went to bed. I heard you. I couldn't sleep so I sat at the top of the stairs and listened. Yeah, yeah, I know. I shouldn't have done. But you can't blame me, mate. Not after all I've done to find you. I know about George and Annie, what they are. I heard them talking about how one day they'd be gone, but you wouldn't. You'd just do what you always do and move on.'

'Whoa!' said Mitchell. 'You know about George and Annie, too?'

'It's not a problem, though, mate. Honest.' Leo gave a half-hearted grin. 'It's cool – you three living together, like. A vampire, a werewolf and a ghost. How cool is that, eh?'

Mitchell just stared at him, wanting to punch him. Cool? That was how Leo saw their lives. *Cool?*

'Sorry – bad choice of words,' Leo back-pedalled. 'But... you know what I mean? You've got each other. You've each got summat special and between you...' He shook his head admiringly. 'You don't know how lucky you are, you really don't.'

'Thanks for telling me,' Mitchell said drily. He looked around the flat. 'And now... I'm going.'

Leo jumped out of his seat.

'But you can't!'

'Says who?'

'Something else,' Leo said suddenly, raising a hand to forestall Mitchell's objections. 'There's something else. One more thing, yeah? You'll like this! This'll convince you!'

His eyes burned feverishly as he went back to the cupboard under the shelves and pulled out a book – foolscap-size and glossy black, it looked like one of those accounts ledgers you could buy in stationery shops. Leo pulled it out, almost reverently, and wiped the cover with his sleeve. He handed it up to Mitchell.

A rectangular white label had been stuck on the front, three inches by two, a near double border drawn just inside it in black ink. And in the middle, the words 'THE MITCHELL CHRONICLES' in silly mock-Gothic letters.

'Go on,' Leo urged, and Mitchell could smell the acrid, fearful sweat that beaded his face. 'Open it. You'll like it.'

Mitchell opened it, flicking through the pages. Each one was covered in tiny, scrawly writing. Usually black but sometimes purple. There were headings – places, dates. New York, Coventry, Las Vegas, Paris, Ibiza, Berlin. He let his eyes take in a few lines of each page, trying to work out what he was reading. They looked like some sort of vampire tales, short stories set in different places, at different times.

'What am I looking at?' he asked Leo with a frown – and then suddenly a name leaped out at him: his *own* name. He read a few lines. It was a story told from *his* perspective. Suddenly, the title on the front of the book made sense.

The story was about killing a girl in a cinema, holding her down to prevent her struggling or crying out whilst… Unable to stop himself, and despite his growing sense of unease, Mitchell read on.

It was grotesque. Thrown in with loads of cod-philosophical musings about what it was like to be a vampire were tales of killings and conversions spread across the globe and across the last hundred years. Most of it was done in a weirdly jokey style – but then there would be sudden lurid, violent passages spattered with verbal gore that made even Mitchell feel queasy.

'This is about me,' Mitchell said to Leo who knelt at his feet, eyes wide and expectant.

Leo nodded. 'D'you like it?' he asked quietly. 'Oh oh – hang on!'

He leaned forward, raising himself up whilst still kneeling so that he could see the pages.

'Flick forward a bit – go on, you'll like this one.'

Caught up in it all, Mitchell ruffled the pages until Leo said: 'That one! Read that one!'

The page was headed 'Bristol' and dated just a couple of days earlier. Eyeing Leo warily, Mitchell began to read.

We vampires usually hunt alone – especially if we're going for the kill. It's partly psychological, partly common sense: there's only so much life essence, or whatever you want to call it, in a person. Two of us feeding off the same victim can leave you both feeling a bit dissatisfied, both a bit hungry. Like the old vampire joke about feeding off Chinese people: an hour later, you want another one!

But tonight's different.

Tonight I'm hunting with Leo.

Who's Leo?

He's cool, is Leo. He's one of mine – I met him at the hospital and we clicked instantly. My kind of guy. The same sharp, acerbic sense of humour, the same taste in music and films – and women too. He used to be in a band, back in the '80s, called Bite Me! It wasn't until Leo pointed it out that I recognised him. They were brilliant. Apparently, the band chucked Leo out cos they were getting jealous of him – he wrote all the lyrics, did lead vocals, got all the women. Happens a lot: everything's fine whilst they're all on the same level, but as soon as one of them starts getting better than the rest, they're out. And Leo had dreams. Big dreams. Even back then, he was getting interested in the vampire thing. Researching, reading, watching documentaries, collecting newspaper clippings and stories. He could have been one of the country's foremost vampirologists. But Leo was thinking bigger than that. He didn't just want to be an expert on vampires. You're ahead of me here, aren't you? Yup, he wanted to be a vampire. And not just any vampire: the meanest, biggest and best. Which is why he came looking for me: if you're going to be big, you need to run with the biggest of them.

The moment we got chatting I just knew that we were going to be mates for a long, long time. And when he asked me to 'bring him into the fold', I jumped at the chance.

There's a bond there — we both feel it. Soul brothers, you might say. The guy I share a house with, George, he's OK. But he doesn't know what I am. And that means he doesn't know who I am. As far as he's concerned, I'm a hospital porter, just like him. Sexier and more attractive, obviously. But just another guy. I often think about telling him, see if he'd freak out. I've even thought about converting him, but I think that would freak him out too much and I'd have to kill him. And he's a mate. So I'm not even going to try.

But now I've got Leo, things are going just great. We've got plans, me and Leo. We've talked about it. Bristol's fine, and I like George, but sooner or later I'm going to have to move on. It's what we do. Stay anywhere longer than a few years and people start to notice how we don't age, we don't change. At first it's all 'God, you're looking good for 30!' or whatever. But then it starts to annoy people. When they're spotting the first signs of grey or noticing their pot bellies or drooping boobs and you're still exactly like you were when they met you, ten years ago, people start to resent you. Believe me, they do. No matter how close you are, that's one thing people don't like to see – a mirror held up to themselves, reminding them, however subtly, of their own ageing, their own mortality.

So you move on. Find a new group of bright young things, a new place to settle down. And you start all over again.

That's what me and Leo are going to do.

He's suggested we try Edinburgh. Apparently there's a really good community up there. He thinks we'd fit in really well, make something of ourselves. I suggested Whitby, obviously, but I've been and it's a bit crap.

Edinburgh it is.

Now I've just got to find a way to tell George.

'You're sick,' said Mitchell, gently closing the book. 'Sick or… or mad or…'

'You don't like it?'

Leo seemed genuinely confused.

'Of course I don't *like it*,' spat Mitchell throwing the book down. It skittered across the coffee table and fell to the floor.

Leo's eyes followed it and then darted sharply back up to catch Mitchell's.

'OK,' he said, palms open. 'There's a bit of guesswork in there—'

'Guesswork? I've never even *been* to half those places.'

'But that last one,' Leo cut in determinedly. 'What did you think of that, eh? Me and you, yeah? Mates! How cool is that?'

Mitchell bared his teeth.

'It's not cool, Leo,' he said calmly. 'You need help.'

'Exactly!' said Leo brightly. 'Your help.'

'Mitchell! You dick!' Annie thrust George's mobile back at him.

George stared at her – it took a lot to prise language like that out of her.

'His phone's off! What's he playing at?'

'Maybe it's just the battery,' said George, putting the landline phone down.

'Who were you calling?'

'Mossy.'

'Mossy?'

'The bloke at work that recognised Leo.'

'Why?'

'He's been doing a lot of work in Oncology over the past couple of weeks.'

'And?'

And George told her what he'd just discovered…

'I've told you,' said Mitchell, trying to keep his voice level. 'I don't do that any more.'

He looked down at the pathetic figure at his feet and felt something stir inside him. Like a snake that had been coiled around his heart, it began to move.

Predator and prey. The line from Leo's stories came back to him.

'But this is different,' Leo was saying. 'Yeah, I get that you don't do it any more – not to people who don't want it. But I'm *asking* for it. I *want* you to do it.' Leo paused and reached for the scrapbook, frantically flicking through it until he reached the last few pages. He flipped them backwards and forwards before thrusting it up to Mitchell and jabbing at a tiny clipping.

'You did *him*!'

Even before he looked down at it, Mitchell knew what Leo was talking about.

Car accident boy makes miraculous recovery.

Bernie. The kid that Mitchell had turned. The kid who would have died except for Mitchell. The kid who, even now, somewhere out there, was living his life as a vampire. One more to swell the ranks of the undead, and it had all been down to Mitchell. He tossed the scrapbook back onto the table where it scattered cans and fag ends onto the floor.

'How did you know that was me? He was a mistake.' Mitchell couldn't even bring himself to say Bernie's name. Even now, he still didn't know whether he'd done the right thing. Bernie seemed to think he had done. His mother, Fleur, seemed to think so. But what did they know? When you're dying, you'll grasp at any straw. You don't see beyond the moment.

He looked at Leo: was he really so different from Bernie? Someone facing death whose only option was a bite from a vampire? Except that Leo was a grown man, a man who knew about vampires, about what Mitchell really was. He'd thought it through, considered what it might mean. Neither Bernie nor Fleur really had. If he'd been willing to… – 'save his life' didn't quite seem to cut it… – *convert* Bernie, then why not Leo?

'Is that what Bernie thinks?' Leo asked. 'Is that what his mum thinks?'

'They will,' Mitchell said, and that snaked twitched inside him again.

'You can't know that, Mitchell.'

'If anyone can know it, it's me. Trust me on that one.'

'But what gives you the right to make that decision?'

'You need to ask?'

Leo slouched, still kneeling on the floor. He looked suddenly defeated, as though Mitchell had somehow finally reached him, convinced him that it was madness.

'You work in a hospital,' Leo said tiredly. 'You see dying people all the time. Can you honestly tell me that you haven't thought about saving any of them? Forget the book, forget the stories.' Leo pulled a face like he'd just tasted something disgusting. 'That's just crazy stuff, funny stuff. Forget you saw that. What about that bloke you mentioned the other morning? The one whose daughter had just got pregnant. What if he'd asked you? What if he'd begged you, just so he could see his grandkid? What would you have done?'

'I'd have said the same thing.'

In his head, Mitchell could see Charlie – a bag of bones, living on borrowed time, and wishing for just a little bit more of it. Would he have said the same thing to Charlie? Really? And if not, why was Leo so different, even if he had invented a whole, fake history for him? Even if he was a stalker? He was a dying man, afraid of death. And that was what everyone came down to in the end, wasn't it?

'You wouldn't, would you?' said Leo. 'I can see it in your eyes. You'd have said yes. You'd have done it. So why not *me*?'

Leo suddenly sank back onto his haunches and began to sob. Tiny, childish little sobs, struggling to get out of a man's body.

'For God's sake, Leo,' Mitchell said through gritted teeth. He really, really didn't need this now. He tried to swallow, but his mouth had gone cotton-wool dry again. There was something about the man's vulnerability that was awakening something inside him again... *Predator and prey.*

Without thinking, Mitchell squatted down in front of Leo. 'Don't do this, man,' he said. 'Just... don't.'

Leo looked up slowly, tear streaks down his face, a drip of snot hanging from his nose.

Their eyes met and Mitchell found he couldn't look away. The soft, pathetic weakness of the man – something that should have disgusted him, should have made him turn away and leave the flat – made Mitchell's pulse race. God, how he'd forgotten this feeling. How he'd never wanted to feel anything else again. This was what he used to live for.

Get out! a voice screamed in his head. *Get out! Now!*

But Mitchell silenced it with a deep breath, felt it smothered and choked by the black snake around his heart. His eyes still locked on Mitchell's, Leo silently lifted his head and turned it to the side. The light was dim and Leo's pale flesh was in shadow, but Mitchell didn't need light to be able to see the veins pulsing beneath the pallid skin. He could hear the blood surging, thumping thumping thumping. He could smell it. His head was spinning and his vision shrank down and down. There was no man, no stalker, no lunatic stories.

No Leo.

There was just prey.

Just blood.

Mitchell's eyes flooded black as he moved in for the kill.

Chapter

TWELVE

'No!' shrieked Annie. 'Mitchell, no!'

Mitchell turned sharply, his mouth open in a snarl, spittle flecking his lips. His eyes were black – coal black, like someone had taken the night and shoved it into his head.

Annie recoiled.

For a moment the disorientation of the jump from the house to Leo's flat had thrown her. She hadn't even seen the two figures, on the floor between the sofa and the coffee table. All she'd taken in was the smell and the gloom.

And then she'd seen them: Leo, kneeling with his head thrown back, and Mitchell moving in on him, his mouth open.

Mitchell growled at her, his obsidian eyes rooting her to the spot.

'Mitchell,' she said again, calmer this time. 'Don't do it. He's not what he says he is. Leo's lied to you.'

Mitchell tipped his head on one side, like a dog hearing a distant whistle. Then he turned back to Leo, gripping his hair and pulling his head even further over.

'He doesn't have cancer, Mitchell. It's all a lie. He doesn't have anything.'

But Mitchell wasn't listening: the blood lust had taken over. He was on autopilot. She had to stop him. After all this time living on the blood from the blood bank, he couldn't fall off the wagon for a lie. She wouldn't let him.

Suddenly, as though an invisible hand had swept along the top shelf of the bookcase, the paperbacks and DVDs began to fly out, arcing across the room, battering the two men on the floor. And then the next shelf. And then the next, and the next until the floor was covered with them, a bumpy blanket of paper and plastic. Annie stared in horror as she realised that it had been her: *she'd* done that. Without even thinking about it, she'd done it again.

'Mitchell!' she shouted – and this time she had his attention. His eyes were still black but there was just the hint of a frown, just a touch of uncertainty. His head jerked from side to side as he looked around, trying to make sense of what had just happened.

'He's lied to you, Mitchell,' she shouted. 'He doesn't have cancer at all. Ask George – he'll tell you. Tell him, Leo – tell him the truth.'

'Fuck off!' spat Leo, his head still tipped back,

Mitchell's fingers still in his hair. 'Let him do it. Just let him!'

'Why?' countered Annie. 'Because you're some sort of sad sicko?'

'Mitchell,' grunted Leo, looking down at the vampire. 'Just do it. Do it, mate. One bite, yeah. Just one. And then I bite you – that's how it works, isn't it?'

'Don't, Mitchell,' Annie said. 'Ask him why they threw him out of the band. Ask him why there's no record of him at the hospital. Ask him!'

For a moment, Annie thought that Mitchell hadn't heard her – or wasn't listening. Like some macabre statue, the two figures stayed where they were, motionless on the floor. And then, slowly, Mitchell pulled back and let go of Leo's head. Instantly, Leo reached up and wrapped his hand around Mitchell's, trying to pull him closer. But he couldn't hope to overcome Mitchell's hunger-induced strength. As though he were pushing away a child, Mitchell shoved Leo onto his back where he slipped and slithered on the books and DVDs.

'It's not true,' Leo shouted as Mitchell started to get to his feet. He reached out and grabbed Mitchell's jeans, trying to pull him back. 'She's lying – the bitch is lying.'

Mitchell took a step back and turned to face Annie. As she caught his eyes, the coal-black sheen swirled away from them. Mitchell let out a long sigh and his whole body sagged.

'Please, Mitchell,' Leo pleaded, clutching at

Mitchell's leg. But Mitchell kicked him away like an annoying puppy and joined Annie at the other side of the sofa.

'He doesn't have cancer,' Annie said quietly, almost afraid to touch him although he was just inches from her. 'They threw him out of the band because he was getting freaky about the vampire thing. He wanted to *be* one. Thought it was cool and glamorous. George checked with the cancer ward. There's no record of him there.'

Mitchell half turned to where Leo was trying to right himself, still kneeling on the floor.

'What difference does it make?' Leo asked him. 'You can still do it, mate. One last go, yeah. And then it's me and you – we can do what we want, go where we want. Just think how cool that would be. Me and you, like in the book.' His eyes, still burning with a mad gleam, flicked to the black book on the coffee table. Annie simultaneously felt pity and nausea. 'You did it for him,' Leo insisted. 'For the kid. You were about to do it then, weren't you?'

Leo stood up, facing off to Mitchell. One minute he'd been a crying child, now he was acting like a bully, all swagger and bravado.

'So what now, mate? You just walk out of here, the two of you, like I never existed? That what you do, is it?'

He came around the end of the sofa and stopped, just a couple of feet from them, emboldened by Mitchell's failure to go through with it, as though Mitchell's strength had somehow passed into him. The light from the kitchen slanted through, illuminating one side of him, leaving the other in darkness. His shirt buttons were ripped, the collar pulled aside where Mitchell had been about to bite him.

'Mitchell...' said Annie.

He glanced at her – and then back to where she was looking.

There was something on Leo's neck, below the line of his collar. It was only now that he was in the light that she could see it. Leo, too, saw her looking and hastily pulled his collar up, trying to make it look like he was just trying to tidy himself.

'What's that?' Mitchell asked.

'What?'

Mitchell gestured with a finger. 'That. On your neck.'

Leo took a step back, pulling his shirt closed. But Mitchell closed the distance between them in a moment and ripped the shirt back, dragging Leo fully into the light.

It was unmistakable: there, on Leo's neck, were the just-visible remains of a bruise. And at the centre of it, two barely-discernible marks. Like puncture wounds.

'Mitchell...' Annie said, taking a step back.

Mitchell sniffed deeply, as if savouring Leo's aftershave. He shook his head, frowning.

'What's going on?' he said.

'He's been bitten,' Annie said curiously, trying to make sense of this new revelation.

Mitchell pulled the neck of Leo's shirt down further. More bruising. More marks. Roughly, Mitchell twisted

Leo round and exposed the other side of his neck. It was the same story.

'How many times have you been bitten?' he asked.

Leo trembled, silently, trying to push Mitchell away.

'How many times?' demanded Mitchell. 'Tell me!'

When Leo didn't answer, Mitchell half dragged, half pushed Leo towards the window. With one hand around his throat he pressed him up against the wall beside it whilst the other hand fumbled with the catch. A blast of drizzly air swept into the room, cutting through the fug and making Annie shiver.

'Mitchell,' she said, 'what are you doing?'

Mitchell ignored her.

'How many?' he asked Leo again, sliding him along the wall to the window.

Still Leo wouldn't – or couldn't – answer. He began to slap at Mitchell, trying to get away. But he was no match for his strength. Inch by inch, Mitchell manoeuvred Leo until his top half was leaning backwards out of the window, Mitchell staring down at him. The wind whipped around him, tugging at his hair.

'One last chance, Leo,' he said.

'Six!' cried Leo suddenly. 'Six! Six!'

For a moment, Annie thought Mitchell was going to push him, let him fall to his death.

Instead, he just let go and turned back, leaving Leo to grab the window frame and pull himself back in, gasping.

Mitchell waited until Leo was back inside, rubbing his throat and buttoning his shirt back up.

'You've been bitten *six times*,' said Mitchell. 'I don't get it.'

Leo just stared.

'What are you? Some sort of... cow? Someone – something – to be milked? I don't...' Mitchell screwed up his face, lost for words.

'That was just the first part,' Leo said after a moment. 'You know, the feeding-on-me bit.'

Annie was losing the thread. 'What does he mean, Mitchell – "the first part"?'

There was a long, long pause. Through the open window she heard the sound of an ambulance, wailing into the night.

'I'm not the first, am I?' said Mitchell in a voice that was barely more than a whisper.

Leo just looked at him as though mentally urging him through the logic of it all.

'That's what he just told you,' Annie said. 'He's been bitten six times, he said.'

Mitchell nodded slowly.

'But to *make* a vampire, the victim has to feed on the one that's bitten him, just at the point of death. You haven't just been letting vampires *feed* on you, have you? You've gone all the way.'

'All the way?' echoed Annie, only now catching up. 'You mean he's tried... tried to *become* one? Six times?'

'Six times,' echoed Mitchell. 'Six times you've done this.' He gestured around. 'I'm the seventh one, am I?' He gave a snort. 'That makes me feel very special, Leo. Very special.'

'So...' Annie was thrown again. 'What happened the

other six times? How come they didn't...' She waved her hands in his direction. 'Turn you?'

'I don't know – I honestly don't know.' Leo's arrogance, his cockiness, had once more flipped over into innocence, and it was all the more creepy for that sudden change.

'And you thought... what?' asked Mitchell. 'That I'd be the one? The one that could do it?'

Leo nodded desperately.

'They're saying all sorts about you, Mitchell. How you're something special. I just thought that maybe you'd be able to do what the others couldn't.'

'There's nothing special about me,' Mitchell spat. 'Trust me.'

He crossed the room back to Annie and put his arm around her.

'You OK?' he asked.

She nodded.

'Come on,' he said. 'Let's go home.'

'You can't,' Leo pleaded, taking a few steps towards them – but pulling himself up sharply as Mitchell turned to him. 'Please, mate. Don't go. Come on. Let's just forget all this – be mates, yeah? We got on great last night, didn't we? Don't chuck all that away because of this. This is nothing. Remember the book? The stories? We can write new ones. New adventures. Just the two of us, yeah?'

'They think we're monsters,' Mitchell said coldly. 'Humans. They think *we're* the monsters.' He looked round the trashed room, with its posters and shabby tatty furniture. And the trashed little man who'd come looking for his saviour – and found nothing but rejection.

'Please,' Leo begged, as Annie and Mitchell left the flat. 'There's nothing left for me without you. Nothing.'

The door slammed behind them, cutting off Leo's sobbing.

Chapter
THIRTEEN

They'd been walking through the rainy streets in silence for a couple of minutes before Mitchell suddenly stopped and took a deep breath.

'This is daft,' he said.

'What is?'

'You.' He gestured to her, arms wrapped around herself against the cold. 'Do your ghosty thing and go back to the house. I'll catch up with you.'

'Uh-uh,' Annie said, shaking her head. 'Not leaving you.'

'Don't be daft,' Mitchell said. 'No point in us both catching our death…'

He stopped as he realised what he was saying.

'Chance'd be a fine thing,' Annie grinned through chattering teeth. 'I'm dead but I'm shivering. How does that work, then?'

'Search me,' shrugged Mitchell. 'I'm undead and I'm starving. Life's mysteries, eh? Go on – get off home. I'll buy us fish and chips. To celebrate.'

'I can't eat, remember? And to celebrate what?'

'Well you can watch me and George eat, then. And if I said "Death" would that be a bit creepy?'

'Yup.'

'OK – to celebrate…' He cast around for something.

'Duh!' said Annie suddenly, punching him. 'George's wolfie baby!'

Mitchell considered it for a moment. The thought of a growling, snarling little bundle of joy suddenly seemed the most natural, the most lovely thing in the world.

'Deal.'

'And get mushy peas for George,' Annie added.

'Double deal,' Mitchell grinned. 'See you back there.'

Annie hugged him – and was gone.

'About time!' George said as Mitchell bundled in through the door, his arms full of paper-wrapped bundles. 'Annie's been back hours.'

'Plates in the oven?' Mitchell asked.

'Plates in the oven,' George said. 'Mitchell…'

'Annie told you?'

'About Leo? Yeah – not sure whether I'm supposed to say sorry or what.'

Mitchell shrugged it off along with his jacket. 'Just some nutter.'

'A nutter who's immune to you lot? That's more than

226

a nutter. I've been thinking about it.' George lowered his voice, as if someone might be listening. 'Have you thought it through – what this could mean?'

'What d'you mean?' Mitchell busied himself getting the salt and vinegar out of the cupboard.

'If there's someone immune to being turned into a vampire... Maybe there's something in his blood that *makes* him immune. Stands to reason. And if *he's* immune... Who's to say they can't use that to develop, I dunno, a vaccine or something. Or even a *cure*!'

Mitchell nodded thoughtfully. 'Yeah, suppose,' he said.

'I'm getting the impression here that you're not actually listening,' George said. 'We're talking about something that could change everything. This could mean the end of...' George stopped himself saying 'your lot'. 'The end of the vampires. If they can't infect anyone else, then they can't reproduce. And if they can't reproduce then eventually they're going to die out.'

'Take a long time for that to happen,' Mitchell said, getting a tea towel out of the drawer and crossing to the oven for the plates.

'So? Ten years. Twenty. A hundred. Don't you see, Mitchell, this changes the balance of power. You need to tell someone about him.'

'And who would I tell, George? My lot? Guffy?' He laughed. 'I heard someone calling him "Guffy the Vampire Slayer" the other day. That'd be ironic, wouldn't it?'

'I can't believe you're taking this so... so... calmly.

I'd be over the moon about it.'

'Well you're not me, George,' Mitchell said, dumping the plates on the table. 'Be grateful for small mercies. Anyway, where's Annie?'

'Upstairs somewhere, I think. Good job she found you then?'

Mitchell nodded.

'That's Google Street View for you.'

'Eh?'

'We found the card with Leo's address, but it's not somewhere Annie had ever been before, so she couldn't do her jaunting act. Said she needed some sort of visual cue or something. So we looked it up on Google Street View and bang! Off she went.'

'Good thinking,' Mitchell smiled. 'Annie!' he called.

Mitchell went to the bottom of the stairs and shouted for her again.

'In here or in the lounge?' George asked as he doled out the fish and chips. 'Oooh! Mushy peas!'

'Lounge,' said Mitchell.

His laptop was still on the coffee table, closed. Just out of curiosity, Mitchell opened it up. For a few seconds, he stared at what was on the screen – and then hastily closed the window and shut the laptop down as George came in with the tea.

'What did we all do before the internet?' asked George as Mitchell tucked the laptop away at the side of the sofa.

Mitchell smiled tightly.

'Annie said that you spoke to Mossy – about Leo.'

'Oh yeah.'

'And that he didn't have cancer.'

George nodded, picking a few chips off Mitchell's plate to balance them out.

'Never heard of him in Oncology. A bit sick, eh? Pretending to have cancer. Not that I believe in all that, but it's tempting fate, isn't it?'

Mitchell nodded thoughtfully.

'Why?' prompted George.

'Nothing, just asking,' Mitchell said and reached for the vinegar.

As he sprinkled it on and the acrid smell hit his nose, he shook his head. Maybe he'd been wrong. Maybe, in the heat of it all, he'd just misread what his senses had been telling him. A vampire's sense of smell was normally so precise, though, so acute, that it was hard to believe that he could have got it wrong.

But hey, what did he know?

'Thanks for not telling me,' Mitchell said to Olive King.

They stood at the top of the car park, once again, and looked down on the city. But this time it was a crisp, sunny afternoon, and, thought Mitchell, Olive looked vaguely ludicrous – this time in a black trouser suit and sunglasses. Funny how vampires only really seemed threatening at night.

'Which bit of what I didn't tell you?'

'His immunity.'

'Oh,' she said casually. 'That.'

Mitchell frowned. 'You mean there's more?'

229

Olive pushed her sunglasses up onto her head.

'You've left home, Mitchell. You're out in the big bad world now. You can't keep running back to Mummy every time you find something you don't understand.'

'You,' said Mitchell pointedly, 'called *me*.'

'Did I?' Olive frowned. 'Oh yes. I did, didn't I? Just wanted to see how you'd got on with Mr Willis. How did your visit go?'

'How did you know I visited him?'

She rolled her eyes – *we know everything*.

'I take it you didn't bite…' She smiled at the joke. 'Actually, your presence here is testament to the fact that you didn't.'

'What's that supposed to mean?'

Olive sighed. 'I really shouldn't be telling you all this. Someone's going to be very annoyed with me for this.'

'Telling me what?'

'Mr Willis. The very special Mr Willis. Did he not tell you? No,' she said after a brief pause. 'I don't suppose he did. If he had, you might not have been so lenient with him.'

'Stop messing around, Olive.'

'He told you he'd been bitten, what, six times? And each time they tried to convert him. They really did.'

'I know that part.'

'What you don't know is what happened to those six.'

Mitchell narrowed his eyes, trying to work out what she was on about. He remembered the brief conversation he'd had with George when he came in last night.

'They were cured?' he asked in a whisper.

'They died,' said Olive.

'Died? You mean *died* died. Properly dead.'

'Properly dead. All six.'

Anger rose up in him at the thought of how close he'd been to biting Leo, and to letting him bite him back.

'And you didn't tell me?'

She nodded.

'That's right, Mitchell. I didn't tell you. You go out in the cold on your own, you risk catching flu. I did say he was dangerous, though.'

'I could have died.'

'Well... we *assume* you'd have died. Who knows. Maybe seventh time lucky...'

'Am I missing something here? If Leo can do that, how come he's still alive? How come you lot haven't taken him in, put him somewhere under lock and key? You do realise what this means. What *he* means. If anyone finds out...'

'The bigger picture, Mitchell. There's always a bigger picture.'

'Enough with the riddles!'

'Oh stop it,' she chided. 'It's all part of the fun! Suffice to say, we're keeping a close eye on Mr Willis. And we're not the only ones. Sometimes you need to let a little fish go in order catch a bigger one.'

Mitchell raised a sceptical eyebrow. 'There are bigger fish than you lot?'

'Oh, if only you knew, Mitchell. If it's not straining the metaphor too much – sometimes even the sharks don't see the trawler above them until it's too late.'

'I'm not even going to ask,' Mitchell said, lifting his hands.

'Probably best you don't. But when the time's right... you'll be back in the water. Trust me.'

'I've told him to ring us as soon as he's been to the clinic,' Annie said.

'Think he'll be OK?' Mitchell asked with a sidelong glance at her.

'Yeah. He'll be fine.'

'Just that he seemed a bit down this morning.'

Annie turned sharply. 'Have you been to a doctor recently, Mitchell? Oh, daft question. The last time you went they were probably still using leeches.'

'They still do.'

'Not the kind of thing you tend to get excited about, medical results.'

They washed up in silence for a few moments.

'That trick you did with Google last night,' Mitchell suddenly said. 'When you came to find me...' He grabbed a tea towel and started to dry up. 'Nice one.'

Annie flashed a brief smile.

'Although,' he said, 'when I looked at the laptop when I got back, it looked like someone had been doing the same thing with... where was it... Pembroke Road.'

'Had they?' Annie said vaguely. 'Must have been George.'

'You think? Why would George want to check out where the clinic he'd been to that afternoon was?'

A mug slipped out of Annie's hand as she went to place it on the draining board and it fell to the floor. The handle broke off and went bouncing across the tiles.

'Oops,' Mitchell said pointedly and bent down to pick it up. 'Butterfingers. Not like you to be careless, Annie.' He caught her eye. 'Not like you to slip up…'

'OK,' said Annie suddenly, throwing the tea towel down on the draining board. 'OK, it was me.'

Mitchell cracked a puzzled smile. 'What was you?'

'Ha ha, Mitchell.'

'So what *did* you do?' He mimed flicking something across the room. 'Go and do your poltergeist thing? Put the frighteners on Doctor Hardon or whatever's he's called? Swap George's test results with someone else's?' He stood back, folded his arms and cocked his head on one side, waiting to hear how Annie had destroyed George's dream of being a dad.

'I didn't have to do anything,' Annie replied flatly. 'He didn't have the tests done.'

Mitchell frowned, not quite believing her.

'You sure?'

'As sure as a note on George's records saying "cancelled at request of patient". *That* sure.'

'Why didn't he tell us?'

Annie shrugged. 'Maybe he thought we'd go off on one.'

Mitchell opened his mouth to say something, but after a few seconds' thought closed it again.

'Maybe we got through to him,' he said eventually –
but there was no pleasure or triumph in the thought.

'Yeah,' Annie said. 'Maybe.'

Chapter
FOURTEEN

'Oh, George!' scolded Kaz as she ushered him in, trying to keep a hold of the collar of a manic, frothing golden Labrador puppy. 'You could have phoned, yeah?' She pulled the demented dog against her ankle and shut the door. 'Biscuit's swallowed one of Esme's crystals, and she says it could mess with the alignment of his chakras.'

George eyed the puddle of squishy doggy poo near the washing machine.

'Go through – Moonpaw's in there. Mind the—'

George pulled a face as he realised that the deposit near the washing machine hadn't been the only one. Trying not to look, he slipped off his trainer and gratefully accepted the wodge of kitchen towel that Kaz grudgingly stuffed in his hand.

'Since when did you have a dog?'

'Moonpaw rescued it.'

'From where?'

'The park.'

'You mean she stole it?'

Kaz rolled her eyes.

'Moonpaw has a rapport, yeah? With animals. Biscuit came to her.'

'She stole it,' George repeated, dropping the kitchen towel into an overflowing carrier bag hanging from the door handle. Judging by the number of paper towels stuffed into it, Biscuit's chakras hadn't seen proper alignment for a while.

'Who's that, then?' came a voice from the lounge. 'Is that our gorgeous Gail?'

'It's George.'

'George? Who's she, then?'

'*He*, Moonpaw,' said Kaz, giving up on keeping hold of Biscuit. He bounced madly around George's legs, rearing up with dirty paws. George sighed and pushed him down, trying not to get anything on his hands.

Moonpaw was sitting on the sofa, cross-legged. She was in her sixties, wearing a 'Frankie Says Relax' T-shirt, a bandana on her head, and a whole armful of bangles and jingly-jangly things. A walking stick was propped up at the side of the sofa.

'Oh!' she beamed. '*That* George!' George noticed instantly what lovely, smiley eyes she had. She patted the sofa next to her.

'Sit down, dear. You need to conserve your energy, you know.'

'Do I?' asked George as he squeezed in beside her and Biscuit bounced around his feet, trying to get up onto his knees.

'Here,' said Moonpaw warmly, passing her walking stick over to him. 'Hit him with this.'

George gawped.

'Moonpaw!' shrieked Kaz from the kitchen. 'Do not hit my dog again, right?'

Moonpaw leaned closer to George. 'Only joking – winds her up something rotten. Goddess only knows what she'll be like when the twins are born.'

'Twins?'

Moonpaw nodded conspiratorially. 'Seen it in the cards. Identical twins. A boy and a girl.'

'How can they be iden—' began George before Moonpaw suddenly shouted at full volume: 'It's shat on the carpet again, Kaz!'

George looked down, and, indeed, Biscuit *had* shat on the carpet again. Right between his feet. He sighed.

'I'd offer you a cuppa, George,' said Kaz, pushing her braids back from her face, 'but Biscuit got on the table and drank the milk. And it was organic. That'll be what's given him the shits. We've got water.'

'I'm fine,' said George. 'Honest.'

Kaz brought him a glass of water and threw herself down onto a red velour beanbag. Biscuit set about sniffing at his poo.

'So,' Moonpaw said. 'We need to start talking about dates, don't we? Unless you really get a move on, we'll have missed the summer solstice. For the birth,' she added, seeing George's puzzled frown. She fished around in a carpet bag at her feet and pulled out a notebook. 'Right,' she said. 'Let's get our thinking caps on, shall we?'

Across from her, Kaz pulled out her own notebook and the two of them began throwing dates and equinoxes and pagan festivals backwards and forwards, whilst George just sat and watched Biscuit paddling around in his own excrement.

This was so not how it was supposed to be, thought George. This should have been a wonderful moment, a joyous moment. And all he could think of was crystals and beanbags and dogshit.

'We could aim for Samhain at the end of October,' Moonpaw was saying.

'Or, right,' said Kaz, flipping the pages of her notebook, 'if we wait until Christmas—'

'Yule,' Moonpaw corrected her gently.

'Whatever,' said Kaz, a little irritably, as Biscuit tried to scramble onto her knee. 'If we wait until Yule, then we might be OK for an autumn equinox birth.'

'Good point,' mused Moonpaw, holding her own notebook out at arm's length to be able to read it. 'Plenty of time for Georgie-boy here to build up his testicular energy.'

'Where's Gail?' asked George, desperately wanting to escape from this madhouse. No one answered. Biscuit turned away from his poo and began sniffing at George's socked foot.

As if on cue, there was the sound of someone at the back door. Biscuit hared off into the kitchen and

George levered himself out of the sofa and slipped between the two women, neither of whom seemed to notice.

Gail was shucking off her coat and eyeing Biscuit with suspicion as he capered around her feet. She caught sight of George and a huge smile crossed her face.

'C'mere!' she said, arms outstretched, and George threw himself into a hug that seemed to go on and on for ever.

Eventually, they disentangled, and Gail, hands on his shoulders, held him at arms' length to study him.

'You OK?' she asked.

George nodded but Gail wasn't fooled. She glanced towards the lounge where Moonpaw and Kaz could be heard arguing.

'It's like *Rosemary's Baby*,' said George glumly. 'When it's born – or when *they're* born, according to Moonpaw – a cult of pagans are going to take it away. You do realise that, don't you? They'll leave it to be raised by wolves in the forest.' He stopped suddenly, realising what he was saying.

'Ignore them,' Gail said with a wink. 'It's not *their* baby. It's *ours*.'

Their eyes met – and the floodgates just opened.

Gail pulled him close and held him tight as he sobbed and sobbed into her shoulder, rocking gently from side to side until, with a final sniffle, he pulled away and smiled weakly.

'Sor—' he started to apologise, but found Gail's fingers on his lips, shushing him.

'Sit down, come on, babes,' Gail said, pulling out a chair for him. She checked that the Flower Children were still occupied and then pulled out a bottle of gin from under the sink. 'For emergencies,' she said. 'And believe me, we have quite a few of them around here.'

George smiled weakly, snuffling into a bit of kitchen towel.

'What's up, then?' Gail asked, pouring them both a generous measure and stowing the bottle back under the sink.

'I've been back to the clinic, spoke to Doctor Hardimann.'

'And...?'

George sighed. 'And I can't do it,' he said simply, and felt himself welling up again.

Gail reached across the table and took his hand and squeezed it gently. 'What's wrong? What did he say?'

George shook his head. 'It wasn't anything he said – nothing to do with the tests. I didn't have them done.' He stared down at the crumbs on the blue Formica table and the jam jar with the dribbles down the side. 'I'm sorry, Gail. I can't do it. I know how much it means to you, and I feel such a shit for leading you both on. But...' He looked up at her and shrugged. 'I just can't. When we first talked about it, it threw me a bit. But once I got over the shock... Mitchell and Annie were a bit funny at the start, but once we'd talked it through, I thought I'd decided. It just seemed right, you know? The best thing that had happened to me for a while. But then...'

'Reality bites, eh?'

George nodded, looking up at Gail.

'S'OK, babes. Really.' She gave a little chuckle. 'To be quite honest, I'm surprised you lasted this long. Don't tell her ladyship in there, but I've been having second thoughts about it myself.'

George's eyebrows shot up. 'Really?'

Gail nodded. 'I love her to bloody pieces, I really do. But…' She cast her eyes around the bombsite of a kitchen, taking in the dogshit and the unwashed pots and the bags of rubbish and the cat sleeping in the breadbin. 'We're not talking about another puppy, are we? Daft as it sounds – and if you tell her this I'll chop your balls off, in the nicest possible way of course – if it had just been me and you…'

Gail let the idea float on the air, before it fizzled away.

'But it's not, is it?' said George quietly.

'No,' Gail said with another squeeze of his hand. 'It's not.'

They sat in silence for a while before clinking their glasses and knocking back their gin.

'To us,' said Gail.

'Us,' agreed George.

'You know something?' Gail said as Biscuit yelped and came racing back into the kitchen.

George raised his eyebrows.

'You'd make a bloody great dad.'

He smiled.

'You too.' He paused. 'Should I tell her?'

'Best coming from me, I think. I've already been

hinting that maybe we should leave it for a while, get ourselves on our feet, financially. Kaz is hating working in Intensive Care – says all that illness is discolouring her aura. I don't reckon she's going to be there for long. And bringing a kid up with only one wage…' Gail shrugged. 'That sort of thing. And there's no rush. Whatever the Witches of Eastwick in there might think. You OK with that?'

George nodded. 'Thanks. Let me know when you've done the deed. We could all go out for a drink or something. Smooth it all over. Ugh!' George looked down as he felt something warm on his foot, to see Biscuit finishing a wee on it.

Gail laughed, her hand over her mouth. 'Give her a week with Biscuit and she'll never want to see a baby again.'

She broke off and George looked over his shoulder to see Moonpaw in the doorway, smiling.

'What was that, dear?' she asked. 'Something about Biscuit and babies?'

George threw a glance at Gail and felt like a guilty school kid.

'It's all right, Georgie,' Moonpaw said, crossing to the table with a decided limp. 'Kaz is in there trying to put her dreamcatcher back together. Biscuit, bless him, decided he needed a bit of Native American in him.' She gave a naughty giggle. 'Don't we all!'

'You should take him back to the park,' George said. 'Kaz said you found him there.'

'She did, didn't she?' Moonpaw whispered. 'Bless.' George looked awkward.

Moonpaw leaned in close. 'Biscuit's not been within a hundred yards of the park – not old enough. Hasn't had his shots. I told Crusty Douglas I'd only need him for a week. I suspect it's not even going to be that long.'

She winked and stood up, checking that Kaz was still occupied in the lounge.

'Now,' she said, eyeing the glasses on the table. 'Where's that gin?'

You'd think they'd be grateful, really, wouldn't you? That they'd leap at the chance to bring another one into the fold – especially when he's offering himself to them on a plate.

But there's no accounting for taste, I suppose.

I'm still trying to work out why Mitchell turned me down. OK, maybe I didn't go about it in a very conventional way. But when we're talking vampires, who's to say what 'conventional' is? But Mitchell seems to make such a deal out of having left all that behind him, of having changed his ways. A new man. So you'd think that after everything I'd told him, everything I'd done, he'd have bitten my hand off. So to speak. Strange, isn't it, that so many metaphors in life are about eating and killing. No, maybe not so strange...

He called me this morning. Yes, Mitchell called me. He said he wanted to meet – had something to tell me. Not that I'm wanting to get my hopes up or anything, but it's starting to look a bit more positive, isn't it? Maybe he's had time to think, to mull it over. Maybe, without Annie there, he's thinking a bit more clearly. If it hadn't been for her, you know, popping up out of nowhere, he'd have done it. He would.

So here I am, sitting outside the Broadmeads shopping centre, watching the world go by. Watching people wishing their lives away, like they're not short enough already. I'm wondering how this will all look when Mitchell finally decides to do it, to convert me. Whether it will all seem superficial and shallow, whether I'll see humans as people any more – or whether they'll just be food.

Predator and prey, just like it should be. Like it is.

Ah! I can see him, making his way through the crowds, collar up, looking for all the world like some kind of outcast. Mean and moody. Well, if that's the way he wants to see himself, who am I to argue? But that's not going to be me. Tall and proud, that's how I'm going to be. There are enough of us skulking in the shadows, afraid of the light. Not me.

'Leo,' he says tersely, sitting down at the other end of the bench.

I nod.

I'm tempted to apologise for the other night, but that would be showing weakness; that would be conceding that what I did was wrong. A bit extreme, maybe. But wrong…?

'How's things?' he asks. There's definite concern in his voice. I can see where this is going.

'OK,' I answer, trying to keep my voice neutral, trying to keep the excitement out of it. I don't want to look too desperate – I think that might have been where I went wrong. No one likes the smell of desperation. There are good hungers and there are bad ones. I'll learn.

'Listen,' Mitchell says, fishing out his fags. He offers me one and I take it. 'About the cancer.'

I'm on the point of stopping him, of telling him that that had been a bit daft of me, but I've got to be careful not to push him away. I've got to let him do it at his own pace. It's got to be his choice. That's where I went wrong, thinking about it. Let him come to me.

'Sorry,' I say simply, accepting his light.

'No,' he says. 'You need to get checked out.'

I frown. What's he playing at?

'You've lost me,' I say.

'The cancer, Leo.' He looks away and blows out a thick plume of smoke and breath. 'Go to the hospital, yeah. Or your doctor. Get checked out.'

Is he trying to get his own back on me in some way, get me freaked out? This isn't quite the way I thought this would play out.

'I don't have cancer, Mitchell – you know that.'

He fixes me with his eyes.

'Yes,' he says. 'You do.'

I recoil as if he's slapped me in the face.

'Where's this coming from, mate? I know you're angry about—'

Mitchell pulls a scowl and shakes his head.

'We can smell these things,' he says. 'Seriously, Leo. Ask yourself: how come I didn't spot you didn't have cancer before? When I met you at the hospital. At the gig. Back at ours. If you were clean, I'd have known it.'

'You really are pissed off at me, aren't you?' I ask him, grinding my half-finished ciggie under my toe. He stares at the remains, pointedly.

'Your choice,' he says quietly with a gentle shrug. 'Just thought you should know.'

He lifts his gaze and holds mine for a few seconds.

'Sorry,' he says, and gets up and walks away.

I watch him go, trying to work out what that had been all about. Was he just playing with me? Trying to get his own back on me for the other night?

It's getting dark now – the street lights are coming on.

I light another cigarette and stare at the glowing tip for a few seconds before I take a long, deep drag.

There'll be others, other Mitchells. I was wrong. He's nowt special.

I'll show him.

Doctor Declan McGough let out a little sigh and shook his head regretfully before folding the paper back into thirds and placing it on his desk.

Life was full of little tragedies.

His bone-china teacup clinked in its saucer as he carried it to his office window and stared at the hospital laid out at his feet. He took a sip and watched an ambulance rush out, its lights flashing as it brought the traffic on the main road to a temporary halt. A couple of drivers beeped angrily, pointlessly, at it, and McGough shook his head again. Too many people wanting too many things to happen too quickly. That was the problem – well, one of the problems – with the modern world. It was all speed and no finesse. Sometimes people had to realise that just because they wanted something *now*, it didn't mean that it was going to happen. No matter how much influence they had.

Sometimes you just had to sit back and wait, let things develop at their own speed. *More haste, less speed*, his wife had often said to him. A wise woman.

He turned back to the desk and picked up the framed photograph that stood there, the desk's only ornament. A photograph of himself, his wife and his daughter. A happy family. They smiled at him from the past.

There was a knock at the door and Mo, McGough's secretary, came in to see if he wanted another cup of tea.

'No thank you Maureen,' he said, using a name that no one else who knew Mo ever used. 'One is quite sufficient, thank you.'

As she took the teacup from him and gathered the biscuit plate and sugar bowl onto the tray, she noticed the newspaper.

'Tragedy, wasn't it?' she said, nodding in its general direction.

'That's a newspaper, Maureen,' McGough smiled gently. 'I think you might need to be more specific.'

'That pop star – Leo Willis. Awful.'

'Really?' he answered, with a mildly interested look on his face.

'Fell from the window of his flat a few miles from here the other night.'

'That's terrible. Do they have any idea what happened?'

Mo nodded sagely. 'They think it was suicide. He'd been drinking, apparently. A bit of a loner – a bit weird if you know what I mean.'

'Weird?'

'Oh,' said Mo hastily. 'Not kiddy-fiddling or anything like that. Just a bit, y'know, *weird*.'

McGough nodded as if, yes, he did know, and Maureen smiled and took her tray away.

'Just a bit weird,' McGough said to himself as he turned back to the window. 'And we have quite enough of that around here as it is.'

It wasn't right, thought George as he reached over to turn the radio up, soap suds dripping from his hand. It wasn't right that he was quite so cheery after everything that he and Mitchell had been through over the past few days. He couldn't speak for Mitchell, of course – he'd been asking about extra shifts at the hospital, which made George suspect that Mitchell was dealing with the Leo business in the best way Mitchell knew. But now that he'd told Gail that fatherhood was off the agenda – at least for the time being – he felt like a huge weight had been lifted from his shoulders.

Which, Annie had told him, probably meant that he'd made the right decision.

And Annie was usually right about these things.

'Need a hand?' said Annie behind him, suddenly, as if she'd been reading his mind.

'Nope!' he grinned. 'Nearly done. You go and entertain Mitchell and I'll make us a—'

The doorbell rang.

'Doorbell!' yelled Mitchell from the lounge.

'Hang on!' George called, scouting round for a tea towel. Annie handed him one, and he gave his hands a quick rub, then threw the towel over his shoulder and went to open the door.

'Hi!' said the woman outside. 'Is Owen there?'

Acknowledgements

Huge thanks to Toby Whithouse for allowing us to play in his playbox, to Albert DePetrillo and Steve Tribe for inviting me join in, and to Simon Guerrier and James Goss for sharing their toys nicely. Also to Stuart Douglas and Paul Castle for gluing some of the broken bits back on before anyone noticed.

being human
THE ROAD

by Simon Guerrier

ISBN 978 1 846 07898 9 £7.99

Annie has learned quite a bit about her new friend Gemma: she's from Bristol, she used to work in a pharmacy, and she's never forgiven herself for the suicide of her teenage son. She also died ten years ago and doesn't know why she's come back through that door…

Perhaps it has something to do with the new road they're building through a rundown part of town. The plans are sparking protests, and Annie knows those derelict houses hold a secret in Gemma's past. Will stopping the demolition help Gemma be at peace again? Annie, George and Mitchell get involved in the road protest, but they're more concerned by mysterious deaths at the hospital. Deaths that have also attracted the attention of the new Hospital Administrator…

Featuring Mitchell, George and Annie, as played by Aidan Turner, Russell Tovey and Lenora Crichlow in the hit series created by Toby Whithouse for BBC Television.

Also available from BBC Books

being human
BAD BLOOD

by James Goss

ISBN 978 1 846 07900 9   £7.99

One of Annie's oldest friends has come looking for her – and what's more amazing is that she's found her. Denise is the ultimate party girl, and she's determined to bring Annie out of her shell. Mitchell is delighted, but George really thinks the last thing they need to do is to go out and meet new people.

Annie and Denise throw themselves into organising a Bingo night at the local sports hall – after all, it's for charity, and what's not to love about having a good time? But why is Denise back in town? Why have Bristol's vampires suddenly started hanging around wherever they go? And why does George get the feeling that Bingo night is going to go horribly, horribly wrong?

Featuring Mitchell, George and Annie, as played by Aidan Turner, Russell Tovey and Lenora Crichlow in the hit series created by Toby Whithouse for BBC Television.